INCIDENT AT WILLOW CREEK

NeWest Press

by Don Hunter

copyright © don hunter 2009

Library and Archives Canada Cataloguing in Publication
Hunter, Don, 1937-
    Incident at Willow Creek / Don Hunter.
ISBN 978-1-897126-41-7
    I. Title.
PS8565.U5785I53 2009   C813'.54   C2008-907091-7

Editor for the Board: Lynne Van Luven
Cover and interior design: Natalie Olsen
Cover photo: Natalie Olsen
Author photo: Larry Worledge

 Canada Council for the Arts Conseil des Arts du Canada   Canadian Heritage Patrimoine canadien   Alberta Foundation for the Arts edmonton arts council

NeWest Press acknowledges the support of the Canada Council for the Arts, the Alberta Foundation for the Arts, and the Edmonton Arts Council for our publishing program. We also acknowledge the financial support of the Government of Canada through the Book Publishing Industry Development Program (BPIDP).

NeWest Press
201.8540.109 Street
Edmonton, Alberta T6G 1E6
780.432.9427
newestpress.com

No bison were harmed in the making of this book.
We are committed to protecting the environment and to the responsible use of natural resources. The book was printed on 100% post-consumer recycled paper.

1 2 3 4 5 12 11 10 09
printed and bound in Canada

For June, always.

chapter one

Liz Thomas shifted in her pew and returned her attention to
the words flowing from Rev. Arthur Hammond. She wanted the
funeral service in the Methodist church to be over. She touched
her handbag, where the mysterious four pages of faded type were
demanding her attention. She had discovered them in a creased
brown envelope among her mother's possessions, along with a
handful of other bits and pieces.

*What on earth could a confidential Canadian military report
from October 1944 have to do with her mother? And why had it
been hidden in a safety deposit box, in a bank that Liz had no
idea her parents ever used?*

The envelope was addressed, in faded blue handwriting, to
"Mrs. Kristin Evans, C/O The Manager, Lloyd's Bank, Cowbridge
Road, Cardiff, Glamorgan, S. Wales." The envelope bore a Canadian stamp with the head of King George VI on it, and a return
address in Calgary. Liz had gone alone and collected the package
from the bank's vault the day before, after her mother's lawyer
had taken her aside and handed her an envelope containing the
deposit box key and a letter from her mother authorizing Liz to
open the box. Her parents had never done their banking at anywhere but the nearby Midland Bank branch, of that she was certain. She had asked the Lloyd's Bank manager how long her parents
had the safety deposit box.

"Your mother has had it since long before I came," he said, "and
I started as a clerk twenty-five years ago."

Finalizing the funeral arrangements had kept her too busy to do
more than take a quick look at the box's contents. "Your *mother*
has had it ..." Not, "Your *parents* ..." That's what he'd said.

Liz touched her handbag, felt the package of papers. She knew
her mother wouldn't have minded her impatience. Kristin Evans
had told Rev. Hammond, two days before her death, "Remember,
don't keep the people there long, they'll have things to get on
with." She spoke in that slightly rounded Canadian accent that
hadn't altered a whit since she crossed the Atlantic in 1947.

Liz nodded her approval as Rev. Hammond caught her eye and

smiled. He was paying tribute to her mother's lifetime of contributions, to society in general and to her family in particular. "... selfless individual ... devoted mother ..."

- -

Liz's son David touched her arm and gave it a light squeeze. Her daughter Bronwen, pregnant with her first child, touched a tissue to her face. Liz's husband Michael sat at the end of the pew.

Liz considered herself a fortunate woman. She'd had caring parents, a loving and reliable husband, and both her kids had survived growing up and had made sensible career choices and marriages, which these days, well ...

"Kristin Evans ... a loving wife ..."

And there were the photographs she had glimpsed in a couple of the smaller envelopes.

The vicar continued listing Kristin Evans' qualities. He had eulogized Liz's father in a similar fashion six years before. The vicar had lauded Gareth Evans as a courageous veteran of the Canadian forces in World War II, a former prisoner of war, and later as a respected and crusading journalist who had campaigned for the underprivileged during his lengthy career with the *South Wales Echo.*

Liz's parents had never spoken much about their early years. She knew that they had been born in the same year, 1912—Kristin in Lethbridge, Alberta, Gareth in Aberdare, in the Rhondda Valley not far from Cardiff. His family had moved to Canada when he was a child. She knew that they were high school sweethearts and after they married they had lived in a small town where no one lived anymore, that was nothing more than a name on a map, Willow Creek, in southern Alberta.

"Report on the Incident at Willow Creek." Right there on the first page.

For their times, they must have been an unusual couple to have been married. Liz had determined that they had waited twelve years before having a child. There had been the war, of course, with her father away for almost six years. But the six years before that, well, problems with conceiving were not unusual.

She'd had different relationships with each parent. Her mother was warm and affectionate. Her father was often withdrawn, detached, as if he saw her only from a distance. She could not remember receiving many hugs from him. Not that he had been a poor father. Quite the opposite. She had wanted for very little as she grew up as an only child. But she often wished she had brothers or sisters. She had asked about that, just once, when she was in her early teens. Her father had continued reading his newspaper. Later her mother said it was "just one of those things" and left it at that. Sometimes Liz caught her father looking at her with a kind of sadness, bordering, she thought, on disappointment. She mentioned it to her mother, adding the thought that maybe her father would have preferred to have had a son.

"No, it's just the way he is," her mother said. "His mind is often somewhere else. You have to remember that the war did strange things to people."

The vicar's words hinted at conclusion. "And in her final days ..."

There would be one more hymn before they moved to the cemetery for the interment. Then the gathering of neighbours and friends at home, with a lunch of her mother's favourite Wye salmon, cold-cuts, and drinks.

Liz glanced down at the tan leather handbag, a present from her mother on her last birthday. She itched to read the mysterious report. It was addressed to the District Officer Commanding Military District No. 13, Headquarters, Calgary, from a Major Gordon Muir of the Canadian Army's Provost Corps. Under the words "Copy" and "Restricted" was the heading "Report on the Incident at Willow Creek, Alberta, on August 30, 1944." A few sentences of handwritten notes had caught her eye at the bottom of the last page. Liz guessed that the writing, large rounded loops, was a woman's. The initial "M" concluded the notes, and then a sloping "P.S." and a couple of scribbled sentences, something about a shop. Also in the envelope was what looked like a wedding-invitation card, two or three smaller white envelopes, apparently containing letters, a couple of black-and-white photographs, and a newspaper clipping with head and shoulder shots of several young soldiers in uniform, including Liz's father. The story was dated December 10, 1944 and the headline said, "War heroes to be repatriated."

She knew that her father had served with the King's Own

Calgary Rifles, had been taken prisoner by the Germans after the abortive raid on Dieppe, and before the end of the war had been returned home under some agreement with the Germans. Liz had found it bizarre that warring nations could be civil enough to discuss and practise the exchange of prisoners.

Her parents rarely mentioned details of their life before leaving Canada. Liz knew only that she was born in Prince Rupert, on the north coast of British Columbia, on October 14, 1945. She knew that her father had been born in Wales and taken to Canada with his parents as a young child, and that a couple of years after the war he had chosen to return with his wife and daughter to the country of his birth. Liz had never met her Welsh-born Canadian grandparents, both long since dead. In their day people didn't just up and travel thousands of miles for family visits.

In earlier years Christmas cards would arrive from her father's sisters and their families from places like Lethbridge, Calgary, and Edmonton, and once, she remembered, from Yellowknife, in the Northwest Territories. She had looked it up on a map and had imagined polar bears and Eskimos. Her mother, who had no relatives of her own, wrote cards back. Her father never showed any interest in the exchanges, even though they were his sisters. Once, it must have been fifteen or so years ago, there was a letter with news of one of the sisters dying, then after that, nothing.

The graveside ceremony was mercifully brief, which would have pleased the no-nonsense Kristin. Back at the house on Greenwich Road, Liz kept busy until the last guest had left. Bronwen and David's wife Kyla helped her clear up while the three men quietly talked and worked their way through much of the remaining drink.

When all was cleared away, Liz poured herself a glass of Bristol Cream sherry and said she wouldn't mind a few minutes on her own. She went into the sitting room and closed the door behind her. She found her reading glasses on the sideboard and made herself comfortable on the chintz-covered settee under the bay window. She opened her purse and removed the four typed pages and unfolded them. She took a sip of her sherry and started reading.

To:
Brigadier J.L. Watson, V.C., M.C.
District Officer Commanding
Military District No. 13
1111 1st Street W.
Calgary, Alberta

From:
Major Gordon Muir
Canadian Provost Corps.

Oct. 2 1944

Subject:
Report on the events of Thursday, Aug. 30, 1944, at Dorney's Farm
(also known as the "Spook House") near Willow Creek, Alberta, hereafter
referred to as the Incident. (For the record: Camp 10 is one of our hostel
camps, a much smaller version of the establishments such as those at
Lethbridge and Medicine Hat, which hold 10,000 and more German POWs.
Camp 10's POW population is 120. The camp, which was established
one year ago, is situated approximately two miles east of Willow Creek,
which itself has a population of about 340. The POWs, most of whom
were regularly assigned to work in areas around the community, generally
were accepted and reasonably well received by the local people.)

Preamble:
It is possible that Veterans Guard of Canada Cpl. Steve Roper could have
prevented the tragedy, had he chosen to intervene at some earlier point
by reporting the events that took place involving Sgt. Major Jack Bishop
and the German POW Kruger and the boy, David Evans.

The Report:
The incident appears to have had its beginning on July 8, 1944, when
the three boys, David Evans, Ian Mackenzie and Pauli Aiello, first saw the
German POW, Eric Kruger. While there is no evidence of direct contact
between the German and the Evans boy at this stage, it would seem to
be as reasonable a point to begin as any. There is little doubt that the
relationship that eventually developed, innocent as it appears to have
been, was a catalyst for what occurred. Much of the information about
the events of this first day came from interviews with Pauli Aiello.

Liz looked up from the page, her brow creased.

David Evans. A relative? One of her Canadian cousins? Maybe her father had a brother who had children, although she had only ever heard of his sisters. Had one of the sisters married into another Evans family, and was this David her son? Liz sat back and sipped her sherry.

chapter two

The gopher stopped its dumb whistling. David thought it looked like a near-sighted little old man as it stood on its back legs.

Heavy rains in the last two weeks had transformed a dry and browning land into a rolling panorama of vivid greens and the delicate yellows of ripening wheat. The colours blurred and blended as the prairie flowed westward until it reached the base of the distant foothills, beyond which loomed the vast shapes of the Rockies. Towering pillars of cloud dominated the sky, tiers of deep blue and puff-ball white stacked one atop the other, like a gigantic layered cake. Between each layer the sun forged a band of brass. Twin rainbows had dissected the sky, one of them forming a complete arch—pots of gold!—on the tail of a brief warm shower.

David guessed the end of the rain had brought the gopher out of its hole. He pressed his right cheek against the butt of the single-shot .22 Winchester. If he shut both eyes and concentrated hard, he could feel his dad's strong, tanned hand adjusting the rifle in his grip, could smell his pipe tobacco and his sweat through one of the wool shirts he always wore. David shifted his left hand forward on the gun's forearm and let the smooth wood rest between his forefinger and thumb. He cocked the oiled bolt and slid it back, and picked up one of the slim brass-jacketed bullets that lay in the grass beside him. He slipped the shell into the breech and slid the bolt closed, pushing the shell into the firing chamber. He dabbed sweat from his brow with the back of his hand and wiped the damp onto the leg of his coveralls before bringing his hand back onto the polished stock, resting a curled forefinger on the trigger.

He blinked and stared down the barrel.

"Nail the sonofabitch!" Ian whispered.

David choked back laughter. Ian was eleven now, a year older than David, and he swore all the time. According to Pauli Aiello, Ian even used the F-word when his mother could hear it. But then Pauli said he had also heard Ian's mother use it herself, telling one of the cats to get the fuck out of her way. David wasn't sure if he believed it. Pauli laughed with his face buried in the tall spear grass that hid them from the gopher.

David was flat on his belly, legs splayed out behind him, like Johnny Canuck when he was mowing down Germans in the comics. An image from the comic he'd read the night before jumped into his head. It showed a newspaper called *The Berlin Blat*. The headline said, "Brontz Munition Factory Sabotaged—Johnny Canuck Believed Responsible," and below that was a sketch of Adolf Hitler, eyes wide and glaring, shouting at some Germans, "*Ach*, fools! You promise arrests but dot svine Canuck goes on destroying our war machine!"

David fervently hoped so.

He squinted through the V of the rear sight, lining up with the narrow wedge of the front sight and centreing on the gopher, which continued to stand upright, twitching its comical mouth and nose. The sun's reflected heat rose in tiny rippling waves from the sides and top of the .22's slim barrel.

There had been a real row when his dad had brought the gun home.

His mother protested. "He's far too young to have a gun, Gareth. The damned thing's nearly as big as he is!"

His father replied, in that quiet tone he used when he'd made up his mind, that the sooner David got to know how to handle a gun safely, the better. That tone always made David's mother mad as could be.

"I'm not Olwyn!" she would yell, which was a reference to David's grandmother, who usually did what his grandfather said, with no argument. His mother would add, "That might have worked in the old country, Gareth, but it's not going to work here! This is not bloody Wales."

But his father got his way with the gun argument. A few days later he walked into the house and, in the same firm voice, told them he was joining the army. David thought that was the bravest thing he'd ever heard. But his mother's face went white. She turned, left the room, ran upstairs, and slammed the door behind her.

David blinked, then closed his left eye. He heard his dad's voice: "Take a slow, deep breath in, let it out real easy, then squeeze the trigger. Don't pull it, squeeze it."

The gopher suddenly jumped and danced a step sideways, before folding like a dropped glove. It twitched once before lying still.

"Great shot, Davie!" Ian scrambled to his feet and galloped down a shallow hollow and up a slight slope toward the crumpled brownish-yellow corpse.

David remained staring down the rifle barrel, the sharp smell of ignited gunpowder crinkling his nose. Ian's patched flannel pants and the tops of his cut-down, hand-me-down black leather boots filled the rifle sights as he galloped the twenty yards or so to the dead gopher. He swept the animal off the ground and held it up like a hand puppet, waggling it at David.

"*Kapow!*" Ian shouted. He waved the dead gopher over his head as he trotted back to their ambush position. "Right in the head, Davie!"

Where the gopher's face should have been was a stew of fur and blood, speckled with fragments of white bone.

David made a face. "*Yeuuch!*" He rolled over onto back, waving away Ian who danced around, jiggling the dead animal at him. Pauli joined him, whooping and jumping about.

David laughed at them, then closed his eyes and scrunched his face up against the blinding heat of the afternoon sun. Sweat beaded on his brow and cheeks and ran past his ears and into his damp, coppery hair.

"You're a bloody sniper, Davie!" Ian yelled, and David sat up, grinning.

Pauli took his turn with the gun, but the gophers had gone to ground and Pauli had to make do with a long shot at a red-winged blackbird. It squawked angrily and flew away as Pauli's shot thudded into the base of a nearby tuft of grass.

"Shit, you couldn't hit a cow in the ass," Ian scoffed.

David retrieved the rifle and removed bits of grass and soil from the barrel and the stock. He laughed as Ian pushed Pauli to the ground and gave him a knuckle rub on the side of the head until Pauli cried out, "*Owww!* Ouch! Quit it!"

Pauli got to his feet, holding his head. His face was red and he was almost crying. He muttered, "What a jerk you are, Mackenzie."

"Takes one to know one, Spaghetti," Ian laughed.

Pauli waggled the middle finger of his right hand.

It would have ended with Ian pounding Pauli into the dirt until he cried uncle, but a distant sound and movement had caught David's attention.

"Listen up, you guys," he said, waving a hand to still the other two. He shaded his eyes and squinted across the half mile of rolling pasture and croplands between them and the main street of Willow Creek, to the east.

A convoy of three olive-green army trucks, trailed by a rising veil of dust, bumped along the road into Willow Creek from the south.

Through the shimmering air, the boys could see hazy details. The backs of the trucks were open, the canvas tops rolled forward off the iron ribs and stacked against the cab. In each truck seven or eight figures were visible, seated on benches fitted along the sides. The rumbling of motors reached the boys, and they heard the pitch change, first on the lead truck, then in turn on the two following, as the drivers shifted down through the gears.

"Jerries!" Ian shouted. "They're going to your place, Davie, come on!"

The trucks were making a right turn off the road, pulling into the Willow Creek store and gas station.

"Come on!" Ian shouted. "I'll carry this!" He grabbed the rifle from Pauli's hands and the three of them ran, bounding down the slope, along a trampled path through the waving spear grass and onto the dry surface of a narrow rural road.

The army drivers had halted their vehicles and shut their motors off. The only sounds on the baked afternoon air were the thudding leather soles of boots and shoes on the road surface, and the quickened breathing of the boys as they raced to get a look at the latest batch of German prisoners of war.

chapter three

Incident at Willow Creek (Contd.) ...
A note on Kristin Evans: She appears to bear an intolerably heavy burden.
It is possible that she feels guilty, even responsible for the events,
although there is no apparent reason that she should. It is to be hoped
that the good news she has recently received concerning her husband will
mitigate her situation. She has requested that Lt. Evans not be advised
of the situation until she can do it herself. She plans to be there for
his disembarkation.

Liz Thomas sucked in a breath. She read the opening sentences
again. Her mother had felt responsible, *guilty*, for what? She
returned to the beginning of the report. It offered no explanation. Just names. The "good news" must surely have been about
her father's pending release. But the *guilt*, the *intolerably heavy
burden ... requested that Lt. Evans not be advised of the situation!* What could it mean?

WILLOW CREEK

Kristin Evans looked up from feeding gas from the single Shell
pump into the tank of Henry Jensen's ancient Ford flatbed. Her
conversation with Sally Marshall faded as they watched the military trucks park under the row of cottonwood trees shading the
store's forecourt. She rattled the nozzle, replaced the hose, and
screwed the gas cap down. She wiped her hands on the front of
her overalls and pushed her thick auburn hair back away from
her forehead.

The truck drivers killed the transports' throbbing motors.
Behind Kristin, Henry Jensen, a grizzled farmer in his fifties,
emerged from the doorway of the small general store. He handed
liquorice strips to Sally Marshall's twelve-year-old twins, Judith
and Beth. The girls were dressed for a day in town. They wore
identical pink cotton frocks that stopped above their sun-browned
knees, and polished black ankle-strap shoes with short white
socks. Each had a white ribbon tied in her straight, shoulder-length
fair hair. Their mother, Sally, a short woman in her early thir-
ties, wore a pale green chiffon frock with less room for maneuvre

than had once been the case. The frock had a low neck, which showed her full breasts and was not quite long enough to cover her dimpled knees. Sally's blonde hair was swept back and fastened with a broad ribbon.

The five civilians studied the trucks and their passengers. Each truck held seven prisoners and a guard. The guards were either privates or lance-corporals. On their summer uniform khaki shirts they wore the oblong red shoulder flashes with dark blue letters of the Veterans Guard of Canada.

Most of the guards had served in the Great War, the war to end all wars, and were old enough to be the Germans' fathers. They carried rifles, some the old and unpredictable Ross rifles from their war, a few the modern, more reliable Lee Enfield .303s. They carried them casually, with no sense of intent. Neither they nor the men in their charge wanted or expected complications.

The Germans shot appraising glances at the two women, then looked away. One, younger than the others, winked at the Marshall girls and grinned. The girls blushed and looked down at their shoes.

The prisoners wore assorted items of clothing. Some still displayed parts of the service uniforms they had worn when captured, others wore the distinctive POW-issue blue shirts with the large darker blue or red circle that filled all but a small area of the shirt's back. The target, they joked.

Kristin examined their faces, several of them speckled with acne. *Boys, mostly, just boys. Jesus.*

One prisoner, sitting with his arm resting on the tailgate of the third truck, was older. He wore a peaked white naval cap, crushed and pushed back on his head. A wave of dark brown hair fell over his forehead. He would be about Kristin's age. He smiled as she caught his eye. Not a bold smile, but tentative, almost wistful. Kristin did not return the smile.

The passenger door on the lead truck opened and a slim man of medium height, wearing a corporal's two stripes on his rolled-up khaki shirt sleeves, stepped down. He had short silvery-blonde hair, blue-green eyes, and a slight smile that suggested its owner perhaps had some knowledge others did not. Steve Roper was forty-four years old and had seen all the war he ever wanted to. That was during the two years from 1915 to 1917. His service to his country had ended when shrapnel from a German hand-grenade shredded his left leg from ankle to thigh as the Canadian Corps advanced on German positions to take Vimy Ridge. He could almost conceal the limp it had left him with.

Roper's shirt was black with sweat. He grinned at Kristin Evans. "Outta smokes," he said. "Mrs. Marshall," he greeted Sally. She offered a brief smile and a nod, and a look that travelled and linked the short distance between him and Kristin at the gas pump.

Kristin's hazel eyes met the other woman's look and held it until Sally dropped her gaze and called to her daughters to get ready to leave.

"With you in a minute," Kristin told Roper. She glanced at the gas pump's register.

"And the liquorice," Henry Jensen reminded her.

"And the gas coupons, Henry. Two dollars and forty-five cents." Henry Jensen handed her the gasoline ration coupons and three one-dollar bills.

"Willow Creek General Store. Gareth and Kristin Evans, proprietors" read the sign over the front entrance. Faded war posters were tacked to the walls on each side of the door. "Save to beat the Devil!" the one on the right exhorted, promoting the sale of war bonds. The horned Satan was a caricature of Adolf Hitler. The other poster displayed a ferocious-looking beaver, wielding a sword and wearing a soldier's tin hat with a maple leaf on the front. Marching alongside him was an equally ferocious lion armed with a sword and wearing a crown. Canada and Great Britain, side by side.

She turned as David, Ian, and Pauli trotted in off the road behind her, laughing and panting like puppies as they slowed to a walk then halted a few paces from the trucks. Kristin watched as the boys scanned the line of German faces now focused on them.

One of the prisoners was a youth in the grey field uniform of the German infantry. Kristin thought he looked as if he should be preparing to go back to school in a few weeks.

"Hello," he said.

The boys exchanged looks. Ian winked at David, then turned his face up to the youth. "Asshole," he said.

Pauli snickered. David glanced at his mother, then looked away.

The Veterans Guard private in the back of the truck snapped, "Hey, enough of that!" and pointed a stern finger at Ian, who only laughed.

The German boy may not have been certain of the word, but he seemed in no doubt about Ian's sentiment. His smile slipped and he dropped his gaze to his boots.

Kristin studied David, the tanned and slim, finely muscled arms, the dusty GWG bib overalls over the once-white short-sleeved cotton shirt. The hair, which she preferred him to keep a little longer than the stubby basin cuts sported by the other two, was the same deep chestnut shade as her own. He was an inch shorter than Pauli and barely came up to Ian's shoulders. He flicked his hair back from his eyes while he studied the Germans, inspecting each face in turn. She wanted to fold him in her arms and hug him, and by doing that make everything right again.

Beside her, as though he had read her mind, Steve Roper said, "He'll be okay." His hand brushed her sun-warmed arm. She pulled away and caught Sally Marshall's calculating eyes as she did.

Roper chuckled. "I'll put him in charge.

"David," he called.

"No, don't—" Kristin started to object, but Roper was already reaching up to the guard in the back of the first truck. "Gimme that," he said, indicating the private's Lee Enfield rifle.

The private grinned and passed the rifle down, butt first. The safety catch was on, but a full magazine was in place. David stepped over to him.

"Remember how to take the clip out?"

David nodded. "Yeah."

Roper handed David the rifle, and he turned and grinned at Ian and Pauli's envious faces. David held the rifle pointed to the sky, expertly depressed the spring-loaded release, and dropped the magazine with its load of five live rounds into his right hand.

"Well done, soldier! And next?" Roper prompted.

David worked the bolt several times, checked that the chamber was empty, sighted through the barrel, then pulled the trigger and heard the neutral click of the firing pin.

"I think we'll promote you to lance-jack." Roper laughed, and he ruffled David's hair.

Roper turned to Ian and Pauli with a military frown on his

tanned, lined face. "You two!" he snapped, every inch the parade square drill instructor. "Whad'ya think you're staring at?"

Pauli jumped and his eyes widened. Ian grinned and copied Roper's stance, his shoulders braced back and his skinny chest shoved forward.

"On parade here! At the double! And put that weapon down," he added sternly, pointing to David's Winchester .22 that Ian still carried. "Weapons experts only to be armed," he added, with a nod of his head to David.

The guards and the prisoners watched the show, most of them chuckling at the boys' performance.

Ian laid the .22 against the gas pump and Roper commanded, "Form up in threes!" Ian and Pauli trotted up and flanked David, grinning self-consciously.

"*Attenn-shun!*" Roper barked, and several of the prisoners in the trucks laughed aloud as the three boys jumped to Roper's command.

"Stand at ease!" Roper snapped, and the boys jumped into a smart hands-behind-the-back position that prompted two of the guards to applaud. "Stand easy," Roper ordered, and they relaxed.

"Not bad," Roper allowed. "Not bad. We'll have to work on it, though. You," he pointed at David. "Lance-Corporal Evans, you're in charge of this squad. Understood?" He frowned at David. "I said, is that understood?"

A Veterans Guard private laughed, "He's Bishop to a bloody tee, isn't he?" and the other guards nodded and smiled. Another added, "Not as big a prick, though," and all of them laughingly agreed.

David jumped to attention again, the rifle at the slope-arms position out front. "Yes," he said, squinting into the sun. "Yes, Corporal, I mean," he corrected himself.

"Good," Roper said. "And this squad is in charge of the convoy while I'm in the shop. Okay?"

"Yes, Corporal!" David replied. Ian looked fiercely at the Germans and squared his bony shoulders.

"Right then, men, do a good job, keep your eyes on them, don't let any of those buggers get away. I'll be back," he promised, and he turned and marched back to the steps where Kristin stood, her arms folded and her face grim.

"I *wish* you wouldn't do that," she said.

"Ah, look at them. They love it."

He chuckled at the sight of the three boys formed-up and maintaining a steely watch on the convoy, their heads sweeping from truck to truck. David's slim fingers were wrapped around the barrel and the butt of the .303. Most of the Veterans Guard members had lit cigarettes, conceding their guard duties to the newly assigned squad.

Kristin snapped, "That's the trouble, isn't it?"

She entered the store and Roper followed her.

\- -

The German prisoner with the white naval cap had watched everything since the trucks had stopped. Eric Kruger, late of Admiral Karl Donitz's "Grey Wolves" — Germany's submarine service, which had the highest mortality rate of any of Hitler's armed services — would have bet that Cpl. Roper often ran out of cigarettes just about here. He had sensed the silent current flowing between Roper and the woman, seen the woman's tension, and noticed the pinch-mouthed disapproval of the other woman with the two girls.

Eric studied the three boys. He easily made the connection between the good-looking woman and the smallest boy, the one Roper called David. Even if they hadn't exchanged the little unspoken greeting, the one that flipped Eric's heart over, the likeness was unmistakable. The hair, the fine planes of the face, and the deep hazel eyes behind long, dark lashes. He chuckled involuntarily at the other two, the tall one with the spiky red hair, throwing back his shoulders to make the most of an almost skeletal chest, and the tubby one who threw repeated sideways glances at the other two and modified his posture to copy theirs.

The boy David was inspecting him, his eyes moving from Eric's patched blue shirt with the faded chief telegrapher's badge, up to the hat with the submariner's crest above the squashed-in peak, and now into Eric's eyes. Eric saw another young face as the boy examined him, a face he carried with him on a cracked and fading photograph in his wallet, a face from what felt like a lifetime away, which he had no idea he would ever see again. As he watched the boy he let a smile reach his eyes. The boy looked away.

Inside the store an electric fan creaked in its perch on a high shelf. The room was filled with household items, dried and canned goods, and cases of soft drinks. The shelves were packed and much of the floor space was covered with goods.

Kristin was behind the broad mahogany-topped counter, her back to the main shop floor as she reached up to the third shelf where she kept the cigarettes. She turned around with a carton of Sweet Caporals and caught the transparent look in Roper's eyes, and flushed. She tore open the carton and pushed two packs across the scarred countertop.

Roper slid coins toward her and as she reached for them he placed his hand on top of hers.

"Don't," Kristin said. She pulled her hand free and stepped back from the counter.

Roper smiled. "I'm off duty at six."

"Good for you," Kristin said. "Enjoy your evening."

"You could guarantee that," Roper said.

Kristin shook her head. "You never quit, do you? I've told you, you're wasting your time."

"Mrs. Whatsername doesn't think so. See the look she gives you? I know what she's thinking."

"I can't help what she's thinking!" Kristin fired back.

Roper grinned.

"And I don't *care*," she added.

"Good. In that case—"

"Jesus!" Kristin spun away from him and began rearranging a row of canned peaches on the shelf behind her.

"Hey, don't get mad, eh? I'm not that bad when you get to know me. I—"

Henry Jensen's voice interrupted him. "Fine bunch of boys, Steve."

Henry was squinting, adjusting his vision in the relative gloom as he jerked a thumb toward the door and the new prisoners. "I wouldn't mind a few of them, come harvest time."

Roper turned away from the counter. "I wouldn't either if I was getting them for four bits a day," he laughed. "No problem, Henry. That's what they're here for. Get your application in and I'm sure they'll be more than happy to come and work for you.

Your reputation as a kind and generous employer is known the length and breadth of this country, and likely by now all the way to Berlin."

Henry's weathered face crinkled and his spare body shook with quiet laughter.

Roper turned back to Kristin. "Be seeing you." He slipped the cigarettes into his shirt pocket.

"Not if I see you first."

Roper laughed and said, "So long."

Kristin turned her attention to Henry. She glanced at the doorway as Roper left and they heard his boots clump down the three steps and across the blacktop.

"Your change, Henry,"

"Nice feller, that Steve," he said. "The Jerries, them prisoners out there, should think theirselves lucky, I would think."

The farmer slipped the change into his pocket. "I'll be back in town tomorrow, Kristin." He winked. "Coupla nice pork chops and some bacon for you."

Kristin's face lit with genuine pleasure. "That's great, Henry! Thank you!"

He smiled, then he nodded, suddenly thoughtful. Kristin knew what was coming next and she braced for it. "They say it'll soon be over, Kristin. Hitler's on the run now all right, eh?"

"That's what they keep saying, Henry."

That's what you keep saying, Henry. Every time you see me. 'They say it'll soon be over.' Every time. But it never is, is it!

"Right, well, keep smiling, eh?"

"For sure," she said.

"We'll soon have him back." As he turned and left the store, he nodded to a newspaper clipping pasted to the wall beside the till.

The clipping was from the *Lethbridge Herald,* a two-column picture over a headline and a short report. The photo was of a serious-looking young first-lieutenant in the King's Own Calgary Rifles. The headline said, "Local man confirmed prisoner." "Survived Dieppe," the subhead read and, under the picture, "Lt. Gareth Evans."

Kristin studied the clipping and reached out to touch the face.

Outside, Cpl. Steve Roper inspected his ad-hoc squad of three. He paced along in front and behind them, straightened an arm here, a shoulder there, then marched smartly to stand in front of them. The boys sucked in their stomachs and shoved their chests out as far as they could.

"Well done, men," Roper said. "Bloody well done!"

He took the rifle from David, did a smart about-turn, and handed the weapon back to the Veterans Guard private he'd borrowed it from. He turned back to the boys, who remained stiff and still as sentries.

"Squad!"

They jumped.

"*Squaaad—diiisssmiss!*"

The three relaxed, grinning. Ian bumped Pauli with his hip and darted away. Pauli chased after him.

"See you, lads," Roper called from the truck. They returned his salute as the motors of the three trucks rumbled and the convoy moved out onto the road.

Several of the Germans waved at the boys as the trucks moved away. Ian raised a stiff middle finger. When they were a safe distance away, Pauli put a thumb to his nose and waggled his fingers.

David watched the last truck recede. He was aware of the German with the white sailor cap watching him as they rumbled away. Heat waves shimmered around the vehicles as they grew smaller then disappeared as they turned onto the gravel road that led to the prisoner-of-war camp.

chapter four

Kristin checked the clock—a couple of minutes to noon—and went to the shop door. The three boys were near the road, engrossed in a game of marbles.

David was preparing to make his shot. His brow furrowed into two horizontal creases and his tongue slipped out and briefly wet his bottom lip. The image of his father when he had sat at the kitchen table, frowning, searching for a word, a phrase.

David flicked his thumb and a rainbow-coloured glass marble shot from his hand and scored a direct hit, scattering the six glassies and steelies from the circle drawn in the dust.

"Shit!" Ian's response flew across the space between the boys and the shop. David laughed and grabbed the trophy marbles. He glanced toward the shop doorway, where Kristin had stepped back into the shadow.

The language was a modest sample from Ian's extensive inventory of cussing, and deliberately delivered, Kristin knew. It was Ian commanding attention, the Mackenzie way. Not unlike his mother, Moira. Kristin had to chuckle at the thought of her. She waited a couple of seconds then walked out onto the steps.

"David," she called, and the three boys looked up.

"Dinner time."

"Okay, Mom, in a minute, eh?"

She closed the shop door and hung the Back at 1 PM sign on the knob while the boys sorted out their marbles and made final swaps. They held a quick whispered conversation that ended in a flurry of see-ya-laters. Ian and Pauli waved to her and shouted "bye" as they trotted off toward Main Street.

She knew Pauli would be expected home about now. Ian would go when or if he felt like it, and Moira Mackenzie might or might not be there when he arrived, with or without one of Ian's various "uncles."

Kristin knew the Mackenzie family story well. They had been a ranch family, not to be confused with a farm family. Farm families lived near enough for the kids to come into town daily for school, whether on foot, by bicycle, or pony. But the ranch families were from the remote valleys and plateaus of the foothills country, many miles back. Moira Mackenzie had done what many ranch women did when their kids reached school age—she moved her three boys into town and rented a house. And she was not the first ranch wife to make the decisions that followed.

The usual understanding was that mother and children would return to the ranch when school shut down for the summer, and the Mackenzies did that, the first year. By the next summer though, Moira had decided that a town life suited her far more than that of the lonesome foothills country and the endless chores associated with the precarious business of raising beef cattle. She and the kids stayed in town. Her husband, Scottie Mackenzie, came in to see them, stayed a week, then returned to the ranch. The two older boys, twins two years older than Ian, opted to go with him. Ian stayed with Moira and neither had been back to the ranch, where the twins now had a second mother, a young Blackfoot woman Scottie had met at a rodeo in Pincher Creek. Moira, a rangy, laughter-loving redhead, enjoyed her pick of robust young men in uniform. They came from various Commonwealth countries' air forces. At the sprawling airbase east of Willow Creek, they were training to become pilots. They had money and Moira had the energy to help them spend it, as well as a generous nature. The ones who went out of their way to use the time-honoured going-off-to-war tune as a path to Moira's bed were singing to the choir.

"This is your uncle Alan," Moira would announce to Ian. And sometime later, with Alan bravely gone to face the enemy, "This is your uncle Jack."

The newly in-place pilot-officer or flight-sergeant would hand out quarters for candy and ice cream, usually with the stipulation that the fortunate recipient spend the rest of the day well away from the Mackenzie house.

Kristin guessed that Ian had no illusions about how his mother and the various uncles occupied much of their time. And he apparently was imbued with enough of his mother's uncluttered approach to life to accept the charity that came his way and not concern himself with things outside of his control.

Kristin worried about the influence the worldly Ian might have on David and, when it was possible and not too obvious, devised ways of keeping the two apart. She knew that to openly order David to stay away from Ian was a sure way of provoking his stubborn side, Gareth's side, and inviting him to do just the opposite. These were her thoughts when David asked if he could stay over at Ian's house.

They had walked the short distance from the store to the house and Kristin was laying the dinner dishes on the good table in the dining room, one of the two large front rooms that looked out onto the wide porch that ran the length of the house and wrapped around one side. The other front room was the parlour, which was used occasionally for an afternoon bridge gathering.

"I'd rather you didn't," she said.

David groaned. "Why, Mom? What's the matter with staying at Ian's?"

"I've told you before. We don't want to impose on people."

David rolled his eyes.

She almost added, "And your dad wouldn't want you to."

She held her tongue. She had seen the flicker of resentment in his eyes the last time—one time too many, she'd realized—she had invoked his absent father. For one thing, it suggested the weakness of her own position, and in this case both of them would have recognized the statement as untrue. Gareth would not have objected. He would have said, "Let him go, he's growing up." And that was what Kristin feared the most, David growing up, and growing away from her. David was all she had. All she might ever have.

"We'll see," she said, and that seemed to satisfy David.

Kristin's glance rested on the picture of Gareth on the sideboard, smiling in his uniform. Handsome. The warrior.

Dear God, Gareth, you didn't have to go. You were twenty-seven, you had a family and a business. You didn't have to go!

- -

He had followed her upstairs the day he told them he was joining up, and she had made the same protest.

"You don't have to go, Gareth. You don't have to go!"

He drew her face to his chest. She felt the rough wool of his shirt, the gentle thudding of his heart, smelled his warmth.

"That's the point, love. I do have to go," he said. "I couldn't live with myself if I didn't. I should have gone six months ago, when it started."

He gently pushed her away and looked into her face, seeking an understanding which she was never going to offer. "All those kids that joined up, Kristin? Most of them hardly out of school? I can't let them do my fighting for me, see?" *See?* The way the Welsh always ended an explanation, God damn them, almost as if it was Moses bringing the word down from the mountain. Gareth's speech had retained traces of the cadence that his family had brought with it from the coal-mining village in the Rhondda Valley. His father, Morgan, had served in the First War. He came with his collier's skills to work the mines, first in the Crowsnest Pass and then in the less forbidding landscape around Lethbridge. The senior Evans couple still lived there, close to Gareth's two older married sisters and their families.

In a rare display of independence, the two sisters, their husbands, and Gareth's mother joined Kristin in trying to talk Gareth out of joining the army. Gareth's father stayed silent, at least in front of the combined family force. Kristin was sure it had been a different story when Gareth and his father disappeared for two hours into the men-only side of the Willow Creek Hotel beer parlour. The old bastard. Always more than ready to step into other people's lives.

She and Gareth were just getting established, too. At least Morgan Evans had persuaded his son not to follow him into the filth and danger of the coal mines. And, she grudgingly admitted, had helped them as soon as they were married, with the down-payment on the store and gas pump. Some would have considered her cynical for thinking that the move was Morgan's subtle way of keeping a hold on Gareth, but Kristin had no doubts.

Morgan had laughed at Gareth's dreams of becoming a writer, dreams that Kristin herself thought a little far fetched, until Gareth sold a story to the *Saturday Evening Post* for the princely sum of one hundred and fifty dollars. Then Morgan jumped in to share the credit when the *Lethbridge Herald* reporter turned up with a request for an interview with the promising new author.

"The Evans have always had a literary streak, you see," Morgan explained. "Poets, really, in the old country." Bloody old hypocrite.

Gareth's next three efforts were all rejected, but politely so, and the editors encouraged him to keep working and they praised his potential.

And now what? Kristin wondered. What would he be like when he came back — *if* he came back? What would *she* be like? Some days she had to actually pick up the picture and stare at it to remember what he looked like. Four postcards in the two years since he was wounded and captured at Dieppe. The first major Canadian action of the war, the papers reported, and fifteen hundred taken prisoner and shipped off to God-only-knows where. The postcards simply said *Kriegsgefalangenlager* and *Datum*, and the last one was dated nearly six months ago, February 4 — Gareth's birthday. Four lines of cramped handwriting that bore no resemblance to his former sharp, confident style. All she knew for sure was that he had been alive when he wrote the card. The newspapers had said that at Dieppe the "valiant Canadians had shown the stuff they were made of."

If valiant was lying on a French beach with your life's blood staining the sand red, Kristin thought. If valiant was all the young men who now would never know a woman's touch. Valiant was just another word for dead.

She lit a cigarette, aware of David's interest as she struck a match, held it to the tobacco, and inhaled. She had started smoking just in the last couple of months.

"A girl's got to have one vice," she laughed, when Sally Marshall remarked on it.

And for what? Dieppe. For what?

chapter five

"For power and land and money, the usual shit," Steve Roper had said, the first time she'd seen him, shortly after Camp 10 had opened the previous year.

Roper had pulled up in an army Jeep and asked her to fill the tank. He signed the Defence Department chits for the gas and gave her a looking-over as subtle as a rancher checking out the stock at a heifer sale.

Morgan Evans, seeing the Jeep, hurried out of the store to reminisce about the other war. He had correctly taken Roper for a veteran of the 1914–18 conflict. He also incorrectly assumed that the Veterans Guard corporal shared his misty and selective memories of trench camaraderie and battlefield heroes.

Kristin left them to it, but parts of the conversation drifted in to her through the open door.

"We had some good times," Morgan said.

"Good times?" Roper said. "I suppose. If you can call poxy French tarts and rotgut wine when you got away from the shit for a while good times. But no, there were no really good times. There were too many good lads who stayed over there. There was nothing good about it."

Kristin walked back to the door and looked out from the shadows. The shape of Morgan's suddenly hunched shoulders told her that he wasn't enjoying Roper's evaluation of his Great War.

Roper continued, either not noticing or not caring about Morgan's deepening frown. "I'll tell you what I remember of actually fighting for King and Country, my friend. I remember being up past my ass in mud and shit and knowing that the next thing I tripped over might be some poor bastard's arm or leg, or maybe his head, without the rest of him."

That's when he weighed it all up as being about power and land and money, the usual shit.

"I don't know why else I was there, when I think about it," he told a now scowling Morgan. "Do you?"

This clearly was not the conversation that Morgan had expected. Kristin enjoyed his obvious discomfort, as Roper pressed on.

"I mean, it's all happening again. What did we accomplish? What did we change?" Climbing back into his Jeep, and glancing first to see that Kristin was still inside, he answered his own question. "Fuck all," he said. "Sweet fuck all." The words carried across the small forecourt and into the store. Roper slammed the gear shift, hurled the Jeep out onto the road, and departed in a swirl of dust.

Morgan stomped back into the store, muttering something about Roper being still happy enough to take the King's shilling.

"Makes sense to me, what I heard," Kristin said. "I don't think he would go again if he had the chance."

Morgan snapped at her, "You stay out of his way. Stay away from him. I don't trust him." He glowered from under bushed eyebrows.

"I serve him gas," Kristin replied steadily. "Gas and cigarettes. In case you've forgotten, that's how I keep this place going."

Morgan glared. Olwyn never spoke back to him like that, nor did either of his two daughters. Just this ...

... *bitch.* She read the thought as clearly as if he'd spoken it.

"Just make sure that's all you serve him." The innuendo was clear. Morgan wanted to goad her into an outburst, to confirm what he'd always said about her, that she was a common woman from a common family. By Morgan Evans' measure, "common" was as low as you could go.

Kristin was pregnant when she and Gareth married and Morgan Evans believed she had planned it, had trapped his son into doing the right thing by her, because that's exactly what women from her kind of background, from families with names like hers, did.

Kristin's father, Jake Lipinski, was a hard-working farm labourer. He'd scraped and went without to provide a better life for his wife and child, better than they had dared to hope for in the barren corner of Poland they had left behind. He had dreamed of owning his own farm and of watching his grandchildren grow, but he died a hero. He had saved his employer's youngest child from a house fire that killed the farmer and his wife and their three other children. He died from his own massive burns. The farmer's relatives back in Saskatchewan took the surviving child to live with them and paid for Jake Lipinski's funeral from the proceeds of the sale of the farm.

But Jake's heroism had not fed Kristin and her mother for long. Her mother provided for them by working where she could, cleaning and scrubbing, cooking for harvesting teams, whatever it took to keep her and her daughter together and alive.

Kristin and Gareth fell in love in high school and nothing anyone could do or say was going to keep them apart. They managed to abstain from full sex until one night three years after they graduated from high school in Lethbridge. It was their class reunion. Following a dance in the school gym, everyone went with their stashes of gin and beer to the old summer swimming hole, where they stripped and swam. Couples drifted away and found their own places on the night-warm grass. Gareth was overwhelmed by his desire for her, and she had wanted him.

Later she overheard Morgan tell his wife, "What else did you expect from somebody like her? Look at what she is." And she had heard Olwyn take a rare stand against him.

"What she *is*?" Olwyn said. "She's going to be your son's wife, that's what she *is*. She's going to be our daughter-in-law, that's what she *is*." And Morgan had blustered in his surprise and walked away.

Olwyn had welcomed Kristin's mother to the Evans' home, an act which warmed Kristin to her mother-in-law. Margarita Lipinski died of cancer a year after the wedding, four months after the birth of her only grandchild, whom she had worshipped.

There had been no more children and Morgan, relentless in his barely concealed resentment of Kristin, blamed her. The Evans line, he boasted, had always been good breeders. Gareth had laughed, saying that his father made the family sound like a stud farm. And he added that the situation certainly wasn't due to any lack of practice on his and Kristin's part, which flushed Morgan's Methodist face and sent Olwyn tripping off to the kitchen to smother her giggles.

When Kristin, employing all the diplomacy she could raise, suggested that the problem, if that's what Morgan insisted on calling it, might lie in Gareth's loins, both the men were astonished — Morgan, that she had dared to advance the thought, and Gareth because he had never even considered it.

"No Evans ever had trouble making babies," Morgan replied, and he invoked several generations of fully occupied houses in obscure Welsh pit villages, as well as his own two daughters who were busy producing and raising kids right there in Lethbridge, as testimony.

True enough, Kristin conceded. But did either of them recall that about the time that David was born, two of Gareth's sister Anwen's kids came down with the mumps and Gareth developed the painful glandular swellings that accompany the disease?

"And you know what mumps can do to a man's ability to reproduce."

They both refused to even consider it.

"It was just a touch," Gareth argued.

"Rubbish, that is," Morgan snapped.

She pressed on. Just to be sure that they were right, would Gareth consider going and taking the test? You know, you just had to ...

And that was the end of the discussion, grumpy petulance from both of them. Two stubborn and closed-minded men when it came to news they didn't want to hear.

Just as Morgan hadn't wanted to hear Steve Roper's "Sweet fuck all" conclusion about the other war.

Kristin felt restless now, thinking of Roper. She was aware, too aware, that he looked much younger than he must surely be. She had once seen him stripped to the waist, waving as he drove by in the Jeep, his gaze as usual boldly undressing her. His body was slim and hard looking. When she saw him walking, the slight limp gave him an even more youthful and somehow vulnerable look.

And she knew that vulnerable was the last thing he was. She had no illusions about Steve Roper.

chapter six

Incident at Willow Creek:
It would appear that the actions of Warrant Officer Second-Class Sgt.-Major Jack Bishop over a continuing period, contributed substantially to the events leading up to the Incident. Whether that is finally determined to be the case, given the anecdotal quality of the evidence against him, and the probable personal biases of the two main witnesses -- VGC Pte. Joseph Kenny, who was located in Edmonton and returned under guard, and the aforementioned VGC Cpl. Steve Roper -- remains for your discretion. Roper remains in detention.

Liz Thomas shook her head, perplexed. She put down the typed page and picked up one of the black and white snapshots from the package. It was a photo of a family group beside what looked like a tiny shop with an old-fashioned petrol pump in front of it. Several adults, a couple she recognized as her parents—my God, they were so young!—and two other couples who seemed to be about the same age as her parents. Four pre-teenage girls, self-conscious in front of the camera, and a slim, dark-haired boy who might have been nine or ten. An older man and woman stood like bookends at each side of the group.

The older couple—her grandparents? The others, her father's sisters who used to send Christmas cards? The four girls and the boy, her cousins?

She turned the photo over and read "Willow Creek, Summer 1941." Three years before the Incident, whatever that had been. There were no names.

She turned to the newspaper clipping. The story reported that Lt. Gareth Evans of Willow Creek, second from left, was one of eighty-one Canadian prisoners of war due to be repatriated by the Germans because of poor health. They had spent more than two years as prisoners of war following the disastrous Dieppe raid in August 1942. The group would sail from Marseille, France, to New York the following month.

chapter seven

Private Joe Kenny of the Veterans Guard of Canada leaned comfortably against the plywood siding of one of the ten barracks huts at Camp 10. The early afternoon sun bathed his half-closed eyes. He shifted slightly at an itch in the middle of his back, snagged the itch against a perfect rough edge and grunted his satisfaction as he rubbed it, like a cow at a fence post.

The army hadn't changed a bit in the twenty-five years since he'd been demobbed after the Great War, Kenny decided. The assholes were still in charge, the mentality still one of, "If it moves, salute it, if it doesn't move, move it, and if you can't move it, paint the fucker." He shook his head, laughing to himself.

Often he thought that he would have been better off if he'd stayed in after the war, become a regular. He would have had his time in by now and be collecting a pension on top of what he was getting in the Guard. As it was, when he looked back over the last twenty-five years—a quarter of a century, Jesus—what had he done? A dozen different jobs, always at the beck and call of *another* asshole, with only the uniform and stripes missing. The routine Friday night arguments with the old lady over the pay packet, and the just as inevitable angry departure to the Legion or the beer parlour and another lost weekend. Their one kid, young Joe, never knew whose side to take. He joined the Princess Pats the day that war was declared. Joe took him to the Legion and they got drunk together for the first time. All Joe knew now was the postcards from the kid that Alice sent on from the coast after she had read them, and which said nothing much after the vague "somewhere in the Pacific."

When the government announced the forming of the Veterans Guard, he told Alice he was going to join up again. He would send her the rent money for the two-bedroom house they shared in Vancouver, on Powell Street, by the docks. She said nothing, but the week after he left she moved to Vancouver Island, to Victoria, to live with her sister, and took a job waiting tables in a cafe. Six months later she was working in the shipyards. She made such a noise in a letter about how much money she was earning that Joe said the hell with it then. He hadn't sent a nickel, or heard from her, since.

He stretched and his knee nudged the Lee Enfield .303 resting against the hut. The rifle slid and bumped along the wall, heading for a low pile of sand that would have made a fine mess of the oiled breech, had it landed. Joe moved, but before he could get his legs uncrossed, a young blonde giant wearing blue shorts and a white sleeveless singlet reached out a bronzed muscular arm and grabbed the gun.

Peter Weiss lifted the rifle, carefully dusted off the barrel with the rag he carried, and, grinning, handed the weapon to its owner.

"More careful, you should be, Joe."

Kenny laughed. "Thank you, Peter. I don't know what I'd do without you."

"The pleasure is mine," the eighteen-year-old former German infantry private said. "And maybe soon you *will* have to do without me, that is correct?"

Kenny grinned. "I certainly hope so, son. Get all you young fellows back to the Fatherland and let me get back to, well, whatever it is I'm going back to."

Then, as if it had just occurred to him, Kenny said, "It's funny, you know."

The young prisoner of war cocked his head. "Funny?"

"Yeah. Funny, as in queer, strange." He propped his rifle back against the hut. "For all those years I couldn't get anything but really shitty jobs and I never knew how long they would last. Especially that last ten years, that was murder, the Depression. Then along comes your Hitler with his big ideas and suddenly I've got a job for the duration."

The young German nodded, concentrating on following Kenny's English.

"Now we have him on the run. Hitler. Once we nail him—and we will—then that's you lot out of here, *raus*, off back home."

The prisoner shrugged, not commenting.

"And that is me, outta work again, see?"

The German pondered. "Hmmm," he said. "But, Joe, you could get the work in a prison, with your—what is the word—your time?" His hands searched the air.

"Experience."

"*Ja*. That is it," the German nodded. "Is what I meant."

Kenny shook his head. "Not a chance, Peter. All those criminals? That is very dangerous work, my friend."

The unintended irony was not lost on the young German, who laughed out loud.

Kenny chuckled, too. He took a pack of Craven-A from his khaki shirt pocket. "Here, smoke-break."

"Thank you." The German took a cigarette from the pack and Kenny lit it for him, using a brass lighter made from a cartridge shell from the Great War. Kenny gestured at the hut. "How's that shit coming, anyway?" he asked. "Bishop'll be along for a look-see pretty soon. Pope's inspection," he added, and the German nodded.

Both of them had involuntarily looked about them at Kenny's mention of the name, Bishop.

"*Ist* coming *gut*, good. Just the *fenster*—windows—now to be—" He lifted the rag he held in his left hand and moved it in a circular motion.

"Polished," Kenny said.

"*Ja*, polished. Sometimes I do not have the word."

"Oh, shit, Peter, your English is better than mine," Kenny laughed.

The German smiled, pleased, then he looked suddenly serious and said, "Joe, when this is all ... *ende* ... finish ... we will be friends, correct?"

Despite the earlier joking between them a shadow of apprehension crossed over the younger man's face as he asked the question.

Kenny studied the boy for a moment, the hesitant smile that had appeared, the slightly creased brow under the shock of blonde hair bleached almost white by the intense prairie sun. A year younger than young Joe, whom Joe figured was likely now in the middle of all the shit going on with the Japs in Burma. Christ, the stories about what the Japs were doing to prisoners could freeze your blood. He shook images from his mind and answered the German.

"Yes, we will, Peter. We will, young fella, for damn sure." He grinned. "In fact, my boy, the first chance we get when this is over, you an' me we'll go an' get cross-eyed pissed, like I've told you." He nodded. "You an' me and young Joe, by Christ. Wouldn't that be something, now?" Kenny's thoughts drifted.

The German nodded, "*Ja,* yes, Joe, that would be a fine thing," he said. "Cross-eyed pissed together."

Kenny chuckled at the broad smile on the German's face, then he turned his attention past the young man's shoulder and along the lane that ran between the huts. "However," he said, "we will not be friends as of about thirty seconds from now." He looked directly into the young prisoner's eyes.

"Right now," Kenny continued, "I am going to be a first-class prick, and you are going to act as if I do it every minute of your life, because our friend, the sergeant major, Warrant Officer Jack Bishop, is about to join us."

He reached up, keeping the German's body between him and the figure approaching from the far end of the lane, and deftly removed the half-smoked cigarette from the young man's mouth, dropping it and his own cigarette onto the dusty ground. He rubbed them into the soil with the toe of his hob-nailed, mirror-shined black leather boot. "Jesus H. Christ!" he snarled, "You call that clean?"

Kenny's ability to reproduce the tones of officious drill instructors he had known was impressive, and the young German jumped, despite the act. His lips compressed as he stifled a grin.

Joe Kenny's rigid index finger was aimed at the four panes of glass in the rectangular window directly behind the German's head.

"Look at the spots on it!" Kenny snapped, and he leaned in close to the young prisoner's face and muttered. "Don't you dare start laughing, Peter."

He stepped back and shouted again, "You must be going blind. That it? You playin' with your weenie at night and losin' your sight, are you?"

Kenny heard Bishop's boots crunching on the crushed gravel path behind him.

"And I suppose you'll want the Canadian taxpayer to buy you glasses, right?" He waved the prisoner back to work. "Go on, get it cleaned. And make contact with the glass this time! Jesus Christ!"

The German youth swivelled and vigorously began polishing one of the squares of glass.

-- --

Jack Bishop's face tightened into a satisfied smile as he watched Kenny ranting at the arrogant young Kraut. Part of Bishop's gratification came from knowing that he would have Kenny's ass later for leaving his rifle leaning up against the hut like that. Two extra guard duties, he decided. Dumb as dog shit, Kenny, like most of them. But at least the Kraut was getting put in place. Bastards have it too cushy as it is. Not as cushy here as in some of the camps, though. Not with Warrant Officer Second Class, Sergeant Major Jack Bishop running the show. They would watch their fucking step, if they were smart.

Since he'd stepped out of the guard room, Bishop was pleased with the reactions to his patrol. He was aware of his appearance, the knife-creases in his pants and his shirt sleeves, and the mirrored gloss of his black boots below the gleaming brass-buckled, perfectly blancoed green gaiters. The brass badge on his stiff-brimmed sergeant major's cap challenged the blazing prairie sun for brightness. A swagger stick, held perfectly parallel to the ground and with the tip resting between the thumb and forefinger of his left hand, was tucked firmly under his left armpit.

Bishop's progress was followed carefully by those prisoners who had been kept behind for camp details while the majority went out to assigned work on farms and road maintenance. Most of the men avoided catching his eye, displaying an unusually intent concern with their chores as he approached. Others, unable to avoid meeting him face to face, straightened up and said a firm, "*Guten morgen*," or "Good morning, Sergeant Major." Just like Bishop's rules said they should.

The Pope's rules. He chuckled. He knew the men called him that, the Pope, behind his back, both the Veterans Guard and the Germans. He enjoyed it, too, but from the terribly mistaken conviction that the nickname had sprung from a respect, albeit a grudging one, for the authority he wielded. The truth was that without exception those who came within his sphere of influence knew for certain that Bishop was nothing less than a miserable son-of-a-bitch who happened to have the power, and certainly the will, to make life most uncomfortable for those he decided had crossed him—especially if the transgressor were a German prisoner—and therefore was best humoured or, preferably, avoided.

Bishop was a shade under six feet with hair that had been coal black but was now shot with grey. He kept it almost shaved on the sides and clipped short on top and plastered down with Brylcream, which seemed, when he was without his hat, to add an odd kind of lustre to his already florid face. His top lip sprouted an embryonic handlebar mustache whose immature ends he was attempting to train into waxed points. He had clipped the right side a fraction shorter than the left, which had a bit more military droop. He kept touching the mustache with his finger tips, as if checking that it was still there. He possessed a natural bulk that in his youth would have been described, flatteringly, as well-built. At age forty-nine, after a mostly sedentary lifetime, much of it at beer parlour tables in Winnipeg and Calgary, the hard bulk of his youth had eluded most of its natural containment and settled in softening pads about his chest, sides, mid-section, and arse. He had been described, in fact, by men conspicuously out of his hearing range, as "that fucking tub of lard."

Bishop had worked as a clerk in a Winnipeg feedstore, until 1914 when, at the age of nineteen, along with his brother James, who was two years his senior, he joined thousands of his teen-aged countrymen in volunteering for military service. Bishop's motivation had much more to do with the feedstore owner's sudden concern for irregularities on the cash ledger than with the defence of Empire.

The military experience was not one from which Jack Bishop emerged with any great distinction, and it was a period to which he made only occasional and usually oblique—if not downright misleading—reference. He carried himself, however, as if he might have been personally responsible for some of the more indelible moments of glory with which the Canadian Expeditionary Force covered itself in the years from 1914 to 1918.

In fact, Private Jack Bishop had convinced a skeptical but over-worked Royal Canadian Army Medical Corps second-lieutenant that he was unfit for trench warfare. The relentless pain in his left knee, he said, was a sign of permanent damage. He was then assigned to work as a supplies clerk at a Canadian military administration centre on the outskirts of London, England. He finished up as a sergeant, due to the inevitable attrition of military personnel, and his own skill at holding the comfortable slot he had found.

His brother James was declared supremely fit, and marched off to battle with the light of adventure in his laughing blue eyes. He was machine-gunned to death while attempting to rescue a wounded fellow corporal from the no-man's land between the trenches of the German and the Canadian troops during the bloody battle of Passchendaele in October of 1917. James Bishop was posthumously awarded the Memorial Cross.

Jack Bishop returned to his hometown after the war, haunted by the secret knowledge of his own lack of mettle, and by the unreasonable conviction that had he, the younger brother, somehow found his unlikely way to the battlefield, the older brother whom he had worshipped would still be alive today. He blamed the loss, and his own deficiencies, on the Germans. Bishop declaimed frequently on the damages he would have inflicted on Hitler and his master race, were he only young enough to (once more, it was implied) take up arms. That being precluded, he was committed to do his best against the Germans he did have access to, and who in this case could not fight back.

Bishop returned to civilian clerking for a living after the war and remained a bachelor until he was forty, at which time he married Helen Smith, a thirty-year-old plain-faced widow with no family and no prospects. He established early on that her place was either in the kitchen or, at his behest, in the bed or, if he preferred, on the floor. He bullied her and frequently struck her. Occasionally she fought back, with whatever was at hand, but without much effect. She stayed with him and tolerated his usually quick, often drunken, and always selfish sexual contact, because he paid the rent and provided food. He bragged to her about his fanciful war service, none of which she believed. She said little and made her own arrangements for sexual gratification. She took a perverse pleasure in the knowledge that her late father had changed his name from Schmidt shortly after his arrival in Canada at the turn of the century, from a small village in the Black Forest. She followed Bishop dutifully to Willow Creek, when the Defence Department's need for ex-servicemen to form the Veterans Guard of Canada was apparently greater than either its desire or its ability to scrupulously assess those applying.

Not that they likely would have found fault with Bishop's credentials. The simple fact that he was a sergeant in the Great War was enough to start him out as staff-sergeant in the Guard. From there, the manipulative skills he had perfected while avoiding active service continued to serve him well. He was promoted to Company

Sergeant Major when the opening arose for a non-commissioned officer to command the relatively small Camp 10.

- -

Bishop halted at the hut where Kenny was overseeing the work-group preparing the quarters for the expected new batch of Germans.

Kenny grabbed his rifle and snapped to attention, facing Bishop. Bishop nodded. "Stand easy," he said. "Sir," Kenny said, and relaxed.

Bishop studied the German, who kept his back to them and continued to polish diligently.

Bishop frowned. "That's Weiss, isn't it? I thought he had been detailed for some work, over at what's his name, the farmer."

"Jensen," Kenny provided. "Henry Jensen. He is, but Steve— Corporal Roper—said he could wait a few days to get this place fixed up first."

Bishop glared at Kenny and waited. He rocked impatiently on his heels and his mouth tightened.

You prick, Kenny thought. "Sir," he added.

"That's better," Bishop said. "Well, Corporal Roper told me nothing of his change of plans. I'll have a word with him about that."

I'm sure you will. And you'll no doubt mention that it was me who dropped him in the shit.

"Sir," Kenny said again.

They both turned as the convoy of three trucks, noisily gearing down and spewing exhaust into the summer afternoon, ground around the bend in the road and headed for the double gates that fronted the camp. A Veterans Guard private on perimeter duty jogged toward the gates and began pulling them open.

Bishop hitched his pants, squared his shoulders, and rapped his swagger stick against his thigh. He adjusted his cap, then spat into the dust as the first truck rolled through the open gateway.

"Right, then," he said.

chapter eight

Incident at Willow Creek:
The next known contact between the three boys and the Germans was three days after Kruger and his batch arrived at Camp 10. The boys were out of bounds. Their presence, and especially the behaviour of the Mackenzie boy, Ian, led to a confrontation between them and Sgt. Major Bishop. The boys were also witness to what seems to have been the first confrontation between Bishop and Kruger, an event that seems likely to have been a precursor of what was to develop among the three--Bishop, Kruger, and David Evans.

Liz Thomas looked at the group photo again. The boy—David Evans? Or Ian Mackenzie? Who was Ian Mackenzie? There now had been mention of three boys: Ian Mackenzie, David Evans, and—she turned back to the first page—Pauli Aiello. There was little doubt that this was at least partially an Evans family group. But which Evans did David Evans belong to? If indeed that *was* him in the group. Or maybe it was one of the other two. Christ! She dropped the photo and returned to the report.

- -

"The creek's up with all that rain we had last week," David said. "Ian thinks there'll be some trout."

"That would be nice," Kristin said. "You be careful if that water's high, you hear?"

David nodded.

"And think twice about anything that Ian Mackenzie says."

"Yeah, all right."

"And be back in time for supper."

"Ye-e-e-e-s, Mom."

She laughed, fluffed his hair, and bent quickly to brush a kiss on his cheek as he left the house.

They met at the crossroads. Ian and Pauli had quit their spitting contest when David appeared. The three of them had tramped the mile or so across the prairie to Willow Creek, just below where it branches off from the Oldman River.

David rigged up a tiny spinning lure, black dots on a bright red background, like a lady bug.

"What are you using?" he asked Ian.

Ian opened one hand slightly, keeping it cupped around a captured grasshopper. He slipped two fingers around the insect, lifted it, and neatly impaled it on the small triple-barbed hook at the end of his line. The grasshopper jerked and squirmed in its death convulsions. Ian absently wiped its juices off his fingers onto the leg of his pants.

David was glad he had picked the painted lure.

He and Ian watched and laughed as Pauli struggled and finally succeeded in threading a wriggling red worm onto his hook. They spaced themselves out along the creek, keeping to the shade of the willows that lined each bank, and began casting.

David enjoyed watching his lure spin back toward him, dipping and flashing in the dark pool he had chosen. Several times he was sure he saw a large shadow follow the darting shape, and he slowed the retrieval speed, waiting for the strike, but each time the shadow disappeared. He wondered if maybe the big fish could see him. He retreated further into the willow's shade.

He glanced up occasionally, checking on the others. Ian bounced the grasshopper's remains off the rippling surface, sometimes moving along the bank a few yards as he let his bait run with the midstream current, then yanking it back and starting over again. Pauli sat with his back against a willow trunk, content to watch his cork float, repositioning when it drifted too close to the bank.

Once Pauli yelled, "Bite!" and jumped to his feet as the cork dipped, resurfaced, and submerged again. Pauli yanked on his line and something flew shimmering from the creek. It flashed over Pauli's head and landed in the grass behind him, wriggling and tangled in the looped line. David and Ian reeled in and trotted up to examine the catch.

It was a stickleback, about three inches long, silver and speckled, and even as the boys examined it, its colours began fading.

"Tiddler," Ian scoffed. He closed one nostril by pressing his finger against it, and blew snot out of the other one. "Here." He bent down and ripped the hook out of the fish's mouth and tossed the tattered thing into the creek. It hit the water and sank, then resurfaced a few feet downstream and floated and bobbed with the current.

David thought he saw the small fish wriggle once, but then it turned belly-up and disappeared in a swirl of ripples where a moss-backed rock broke the surface.

"You prob'ly killed it," Pauli said.

"So what?" Ian turned on him.

Pauli shrugged. "I coulda just put it back." He picked up the line and hook and wiped some blood and specks of slime from the barbs.

"Anyway they're not biting," Ian announced. "Let's pack it in."

David added, "I think it's too hot for them. They're staying deep."

Ian and Pauli nodded, apparently impressed with the assessment.

"So what do you want to do?" David said.

"We could ride old man Krowsky's pony," Pauli suggested. "He's gone into town."

Thomas Krowsky was a widower who lived alone on a small mixed-farm a mile out of Willow Creek. He kept a Shetland Pony for the rare visits made by his grandchildren living in Vancouver. There was always a halter conveniently left by the gate or on the fence.

"Okay," David agreed.

But Ian nixed the idea. "Nah, shit. I don't wanna ride today." He grinned. "I wanna see them new Krauts. Let's go to the camp." He looked at David, who saw a challenge in the green eyes set in the wildly freckled face beneath a stubble of red hair.

"I'm not supposed to," David said. He felt a blush rising as Ian's eyes said he had correctly guessed what David's answer would be.

Ian laughed and affected a whining echo of David's answer. "'I'm not supposed to ... I'm not supposed to.'" He lost his smile. "Shit, Davie, nobody's *supposed* to. Well, don't, then, if you're scared."

He walked back to his fishing gear and started packing it. "I'm goin', anyway. Who's gonna know?" he said, as he reeled in his line and snagged the hook onto the reel. He jerked a thumb at Pauli. "You're comin', aren't you?"

Pauli picked his nose with an index finger and wiped the product on his coveralls. He looked from Ian to David, then shrugged. "Yeah, I guess." He began sorting his fishing gear.

"Right, well let's go." Ian laid his rod across his shoulder, turned, and walked away. Pauli grabbed his stuff and started after him.

"See you later, Davie, eh?" Pauli said.

They had reached a low hanging willow at the first bend in the creek. David dug his toe into the ground and scuffed up some grass and soil as he watched them. Pauli's chubby body swayed as he hurried to keep up with Ian. Pauli would be sweating; it would be rolling down his neck and into the little creases he had around his chin. David's mother said it was just baby fat that would firm up. Ian said that his mother said it was from eating all that spaghetti. David rolled some spit around under his tongue then pursed his lips and aimed the spit out and down at the ground. A small string of it sprang back and dribbled onto his chin. He wiped it off with his bare arm. Ian now was out of sight around the bend, Pauli just behind him.

"And don't be going near that camp." How many times had his mom said that?

Lots.

But what was wrong with it? Ian said he'd been there plenty of times and nothing had happened. Maybe he had. And Pauli was going.

Pauli's rear end went from sight.

"Hey!" David shouted. "Ian, all right, wait up!"

He picked up his fishing rod and made the lure fast to the reel and trotted along the footpath, faintly worn into the grass along the creek bank.

He had reached the willow tree when Ian reappeared, a grin splitting his face and showing the large gap between his upper front teeth. Ian punched David on the shoulder. "Come on, you dope," he said, and David laughed along with him.

- -

The three boys cantered toward the crest of a long, grassy slope. Ian led the way, followed by David, with Pauli at the rear. The tips of their Eaton's catalogue fishing rods dipped and wobbled as they jumped over bumps and into hollows.

"Commandos," David said, puffing slightly as Ian stepped up

the pace. He lengthened his stride to keep up with him. "I'm going to join the commandos if the war's still on."

"Spitfires are best," Ian countered. "I've got two uncles flying Spitfires and they go like bats out of hell."

David pictured black winged shapes zooming out of a deep pit filled with fire, and was impressed.

"Hah, they're not really your uncles," Pauli panted from his spot at the rear. "Everybody knows that."

Ian spun round on him, glaring down from the additional height advantage supplied by his lead position on the slope.

"Shut up, fatso, or I'll knock your teeth down your throat." Then he laughed. "Anyway," he said. "You're a friggin' Eye-tie—what do you know? Mussolini with shit for brains."

Pauli's plump cheeks reddened and he looked away.

They had reached a painted wooden sign nailed to two two-by-four stakes in the ground. In big black letters across the top was Department of National Defence, and below that, in bright red against the white background, No Admittance. Keep Out.

Ian gave the sign the finger.

A few steps took them to the top of the hill, where they looked down across the wire fence and into the compound of Camp 10.

Ian pointed. "There they are! Let's go." He started at a run down the slope leading to the perimeter fence. Pauli followed him. David hesitated just a second before launching himself after them.

chapter nine

Liz Thomas got up from the settee and poured herself another
glass of sherry. At the sideboard she glanced in the mirror. She
was fairly satisfied with what she saw. Not bad, for her age. A few
lines around the eyes, creases beginning at the side of the mouth,
all of which her husband Michael gallantly insisted were signs of
strengthening character as much as maturing years. Such a fine
man, really. It had always hurt her that her father never found the
time to become real friends with Michael, especially given their
common service background. Michael was a young sergeant in the
Parachute Regiment when Liz first met him, in the mid-sixties.
On being introduced, her father had said curtly, "I was a commis-
sioned officer myself." Once, after they were married and a few
days before Michael was to leave for a three-month duty tour in
Asia, Liz's father had said, "I'll keep an eye on her," in a tone that
she found hard to define. Not warm, certainly. She had dismissed
it as just another of his odd ways. It never happened again because
Michael left the army and started what would become a success-
ful landscaping business. She picked up a framed colour picture of
her mother taken sometime in the fifties. The slightly upturned
nose that Liz had inherited, the rich auburn hair that Liz decidedly had not inherited, and the penetrating dark eyes. Liz wondered which branch of the genealogical tree had given her blonde
hair and eyes that Michael said reminded him of the turquoise
depths of the Caribbean, which he had never visited.

- -

The new arrivals had had two days to settle in. Their introduc-
tion to the camp commander, Sergeant Major Jack Bishop, had
been brief, before he had left for a two-day Command meeting in
Calgary. Today Bishop was back.

The prisoners stood in three loose ranks of seven, facing

Corporal Steve Roper. In the front rank, Eric Kruger listened to a youth standing beside him. The boy wore a tattered tunic with the insignia and wings of a sergeant-pilot in the Luftwaffe, the German air force.

"*Ist besser,*" the young flyer said.

Better than the huge Lethbridge camp where they had been lodged previously, he meant. Eric Kruger nodded. "*Ja, viel besser.*" Much better. *And a hell of a lot safer.*

Roper marshalled the Germans into a semblance of order. "Listen up." He spoke particularly to Eric Kruger, who had the best grip on the language. The sailor nodded, accepting the role of translator.

Roper pointed his thumb toward the camp's company office, just outside the compound, where Bishop had appeared in the doorway. "The Sergeant Major."

Eric Kruger spoke in German, and heads nodded.

Roper said, "Your Kommandant," and a few smiles appeared. "When the Kommandant says jump, you ask, 'How high, sir?'"

Eric Kruger told them in German. The prisoners laughed. *The more things changed ...*

"Do that and you'll have no trouble," Roper said.

Eric Kruger translated. "They understand," he said. He had not sought the role of spokesman. Like most everything else in the military, it just happened. He had learned long ago the simple rules, like don't volunteer unless you know exactly what's in store, and admit to nothing. In basic training a favourite of the instructors was to ask whether there were any musicians among the rookies. The *dumkopfs* who waved their ingratiating hands were told, good, step this way, we've got three pianos that need moving.

You kept your mouth shut and made the best of it.

He studied Bishop, who had arrived and now stood next to Roper, examining the prisoners. He looked away when Bishop's gaze reached him.

Roper turned to Bishop and snapped smartly to attention. "New men, sir. All present and correct."

Bishop inspected Roper, who had one more button undone on his shirt than the regulations for summertime shirt-sleeve-order demanded. His shirt was rumpled at the waist where he had failed to tuck it neatly back into his pants.

Bishop said, "You look like shit, Corporal."

Roper remained silent. He stared past Bishop's shoulders and directly into the face of his drinking buddy and friend, Joe Kenny, who grinned and shook his head in sympathy.

The prisoners watched with varying degrees of interest. Eric Kruger heard every word, his senses honed through years of close contact with such men, both in the peacetime merchant navy and since in the war. He placed Bishop high on his list of people to avoid.

Bishop examined them, stopping whenever a man shuffled, fixing him with a glare until the culprit stood still.

Finally, "Well, Corporal, what will we do with this lot?"

Roper, having heard the same question on several previous occasions, treated it as he had learned to, as rhetorical. And next, he thought, *What a bloody shower.*

"What a bloody shower. Aren't they, Corporal?"

Roper responded with the safely neutral, "Sir," which Bishop accepted as agreement.

"Pathetic."

Roper sighed audibly. Bishop snapped his head around. "Something to add, Corporal?"

Roper considered the question only briefly before shaking his head. "No, sir."

A shout of laughter from outside the perimeter wire turned their heads. The three boys had been halfway down the incline toward the wire fence when Ian tripped, fell, and slid the rest of the way to the bottom. He was on all fours, his head cocked, gazing through the wire-mesh squares like a large red-headed dog. The laughter was from David and Pauli, who had stumbled their way down to land beside him.

"Jesus Christ!" Bishop marched toward the fence. "What the hell do you think you're doing here?" He lashed his swagger stick in the air. "You're out of bloody bounds!"

Ian jumped to his feet. He shaped himself into a pose that was almost more Bishop than Bishop was. Using his fishing pole as a waggly swagger stick, and in a remarkably accurate impersonation of the sergeant major, including the smattering of Cockney with which Bishop frequently would try to entertain an audience, Ian turned to David and Pauli and barked, "So piss orf 'ome, orright?"

David and Pauli were as good as the occasion. They snapped to attention, saluted, and said smartly, "Yes, sir!"

Even Bishop's beefy face quivered, on the verge of a chuckle, as Ian nodded and gesticulated his satisfaction at his troops, copying the sergeant major's facial and body gestures. The Germans chuckled, and Roper and Joe Kenny ducked their heads to hide their laughter.

But Bishop's grudging amusement was short lived. "Little sods," he said. "Right, you've had your fun, now bugger off."

The boys glanced at each other, and Ian laughed.

Bishop glared. "Go on, when I tell you!"

Ian made no move to leave. Instead he hawked and cleared the back of his nose and throat and shot a fat glob of phlegm, which landed and hung on the bottom strand of wire. He wiped an overflow off his nose with a finger and flicked it onto the grass. "When we're ready to," he said as he folded his arms and stared back at Bishop.

Ian's cheeky pose raised a rattle of laughter from the German ranks.

Joe Kenny laughed. "Little bugger!"

Bishop's face flushed. He lowered his swagger stick from its assigned place under his arm. He pointed the tip of the stick at Ian and moved it back and forth to include David and Pauli. "If you're not gone when I'm through with this lot," he gestured to the prisoner ranks, "I'll tan the skin off your arses. And that's a promise."

Ian laughed. "You'll have to catch us first!"

Bishop lashed at the wire with his swagger stick as Ian danced backwards.

"You little—!" Then he had to duck as the swagger stick bounced back of the fence and almost caught him in the face. He heard the laughter from the prisoners and as he turned saw the ranks losing formation.

He swung back to face the boys. "I'll deal with you later." He turned and marched back to the prisoners. "Get back in formation! Corporal!"

The Germans needed no interpreter. They were quickly back in ranks.

Bishop glared at Roper then faced the Germans, who were

perfectly still. "We were interrupted." He marched slowly along the front line, stopped, did a sharp about-turn, and walked back. He stood in an upright, at-ease position, swagger stick back in place, and stared at the Germans from under his hat brim.

Roper counted the timed pause. *One, two, three....*

"My name is Bishop."

Another pause, while Bishop engaged eyes up and down the ranks. Heads nodded.

"Sergeant Major Bishop." His chin tipped up slightly.

"I run this camp."

Feet shuffled.

"Is that clear?"

The question was as much a threat.

The three boys watched, their attention skipping from Bishop to the Germans, to Roper and Kenny, and back to Bishop.

"Is that clear?" Louder this time.

Frowns creased some prisoner faces.

"Do you understand?"

Prisoners exchanged looks, and heads turned toward Eric Kruger.

Bishop said, "*Verstehen sie?* Jesus!"

Anxiety now on some faces in the ranks as Bishop railed. Then, "We understand, Sergeant Major."

The almost-perfect English startled Bishop. He searched the German ranks for the source and found it.

Outside the fence the boys moved closer to the wire. David saw that the prisoner who had answered was the one who had watched him from the back of the truck when they were at the gas pump, the one with the sailor hat. And Bishop didn't seem too pleased with him, although he had answered Bishop's question. David studied the German. The man was taller than he had seemed when he was sitting in the truck. He was at eye-level with Bishop, who was now talking back at him. The words came clearly across the parade area.

"Well, that's nice," Bishop said. "As long as we understand each other." He stroked his broad chin, fingered bits of his mustache. "And we speak the King's English, by George." He grinned at what he considered a clever pun, which he had appropriated from a cartoon in the *Calgary Herald.* "How do we manage that, then?"

Bishop's voice dripped false geniality. Eric Kruger's explanation was careful, and brief.

"Passenger ships, Sergeant Major. Liverpool, Montreal, New York—I am a sailor."

Roper watched Bishop consider the response. Bishop smiled, that smile, and shook his head slowly. "No, Fritz. You are not a sailor."

Steve Roper sighed. The German had given the miserable bugger an opening. Least said, the best, always. The sailor looked like he realized that now.

Bishop's superficially chiding tone commanded the prisoners' attention, as well as that of the three boys, whom it now seemed Bishop was content to let remain as an audience.

"I will tell you what you are." He paced now as he spoke. Four steps along the front rank, to the right, a swivel, four steps back, halt. He shrugged, dismissive, contemptuous.

"You are *nothing*. You are a *number*." He stared at the sailor, who met his eyes briefly then looked away. "Nothing more," Bishop said. He looked at Roper as though for confirmation. Roper examined his boots. Joe Kenny focused on something distant.

"We have to feed you," Bishop said. "And we have to see that you don't run away." He lifted his hand and wiped away a trickle of sweat that had escaped from under his hat band. "And you," he said, "you have to watch your step!" He slapped his swagger stick against his left leg. "Because if you don't," he paused and scanned all the faces, "If you don't, I'll *have* you." His smile at Eric Kruger was rich with promise. "That's simple enough, isn't it?"

The smile served only to enhance Eric Kruger's sense of danger. He nodded. "Yes, Sergeant Major."

"Very good," Bishop said. "Three little words: yes, Sergeant Major. Keep them handy." His gaze lingered on the German, then he turned to speak to Roper. He froze in his half-turned position at the sound of stifled laughter from the prisoner ranks. Behind Eric Kruger an infantry private stood with his lips too tightly compressed, his eyes and face blank. Next to Eric Kruger, the young sergeant-pilot failed to erase the smile caused by a comment that had come from behind him.

Bishop examined the youth.

Eric Kruger watched Bishop, who now seemed oddly pleased

rather than angry at the interruption. Under the waxed mustache, a smile touched his lips. Eric Kruger recognized this as a very bad sign.

Bishop tapped his swagger stick rhythmically against the gaiter around his right lower leg as he considered what he had before him.

The young German pilot had brought himself under control. He stood to attention, his eyes focused on Bishop's cap badge, avoiding the Sergeant Major's eyes.

"Well, what do we have here?" Bishop raised his swagger stick and rested it on the swastika sewn to the youth's ragged blue-grey tunic. "Flyer boy, is it?"

The youth's brow creased as he struggled to understand, and then he smiled.

Bishop returned the smile. He stretched his arms out and started waggling them, like a child playing airplanes. "Pilot?" Bishop said. "Flyer?"

Several of the Germans chuckled at Bishop's performance.

Eric Kruger glanced across at Steve Roper. The corporal was not smiling. He watched Bishop with some concern.

The young pilot relaxed. He grinned and nodded concurrence with Bishop's playful mime. "*Ja,*" he agreed, "*Ich bin ein Flieger—ein pilot.*"

Bishop brought his arms slowly down to his sides. He was no longer smiling. He tapped a slow measure with his stick, nodding his head with each tap, as though reaching a decision. Suddenly the tip of the stick whipped up like a striking cobra and struck the boy a darting blow in the chest. The young German took an involuntary step back, bewildered at the sea-change in Bishop's attitude.

"*Vas?*" he began.

"You little shit."

The boy shook his head, alarmed now. "*Vas ist?*"

"The Hun in the sun, were you?"

The boy was lost. He shrugged, gave a helpless smile. "*Ich spreche nicht Englisch—*" he started, but Bishop stepped on the words before they were out.

"How many good boys did you put away? Enjoy it, did you? What, Messerschmitts, was it? Always from behind, the Hun in the sun, right?"

The boy was puzzled, and worried.

"You little Nazi shit!"

Sounds of protest rose in the German ranks.

Roper exchanged a look with Joe Kenny. Kenny shook his head.

"Never knows when to stop."

The boy-pilot's eyes widened. *"Nein! Ich bin nicht Nazi! Ich bin—"*

"Nicht Nazi, my ass!" Bishop roared. His face was a rising red tide.

Eric Kruger spoke up. "He is not a Nazi, Sergeant Major."

Bishop stopped in mid-breath. He turned his head, slowly, and settled his gaze on the sailor.

- -

Eric Kruger knew who the Nazis were, the zealots who despite all news from Europe to the contrary still preached that Adolf Hitler would yet ride triumphant into the POW camp in his long, shiny Volkswagen and deliver them unto the Fatherland.

At the end of Eric Kruger's first month in the sprawling Lethbridge camp with its 10,000-plus prisoners, two young infantrymen, farm boys before the war, refused to swear allegiance to the swastika fanatics. They were judged, sentenced, and executed by being hanged from ceiling struts in the barracks communal showers. It was made to look like suicide, including the "discovery" of a note indicating the deaths were a pact between two homosexual lovers. Eric challenged the ring leaders, and was warned that unless he kept his mouth shut and his suspicions to himself, he would be the next to dance on the end of a rope. Wisely he concluded that the "unless" was delivered as a distraction and that regardless, he was marked for execution. He requested and was quickly granted a transfer by a Veterans Guard administration that suspected but had no hope of proving what had transpired.

- -

As Bishop eyed him now, Eric Kruger briefly wondered if he might have gone from bad to worse, frying pan to fire, as his English shipmates used to say. But no. Bishop was dangerous, but not in the certain, terminal way the Death's Head S.S. thugs were. Bishop was probably avoidable, if one kept his mouth shut. He must remember that.

Eric Kruger's thoughts, and Bishop's attention, were diverted once again by Ian Mackenzie.

"Hey, lookit!"

Heads turned.

Using a gob of spit worked into a pinch of soil in the palm of his hand, Ian had formed a paste which he spread under his freckled nose in a duplicate of the toothbrush mustache favoured by the German Chancellor.

As all eyes found him, Ian flung his right arm out straight in the familiar Nazi salute and turned his face with its now glaring eyes toward them. He goose-stepped along a ten-stride length of the fence, executed a spinning turn, and marched back. He had persuaded a few stray, longer hairs from the front of his head to lie down flat on his brow and slanted in the style worn by Hitler. He was the wrong size, his hair the wrong colour, and his mustache a patch of mud, but he was remarkably able to evoke the figure of Adolf Hitler that the boys and the Veterans Guard knew from the movie newsreels, and some of the Germans from personal witness.

Roper and Kenny swapped grins. The Mackenzie kid was hopeless, incorrigible. And comical. Most prisoners seemed to share the thought, shaking their heads and laughing as Ian continued his lone parade.

David watched the sailor, who wore an odd little smile, sort of funny and sad at the same time, he thought. The sailor caught David's eyes on him and his smile broadened, and after a second David realized it was because he had been smiling back at the German's smile without realizing it. He put his face back straight and the sailor sort of cocked his eyebrows, like a question—where did the smile go?—then the German nodded just a little bit, as though David had said something and he was agreeing with it, though David couldn't think what it could have been.

Eric Kruger watched David examine him while the red-headed one did his Hitler mimicry, and he was pleased when David appeared to return his smile, even though a small and slightly puzzled frown soon recaptured the boy's face. The reactions reminded Eric painfully of the boy and the young woman in the photograph in his wallet, for whom he prayed daily, hoping that in the unlikely chance that there was a God among all the nightmares of the last five years, He would spare them a thought.

Bishop caught the silent exchange between young Evans and the mouthy sailor. It both puzzled and angered him. But Mackenzie was the one he wanted.

"You!" Bishop yelled, striding toward the fence and aiming his swagger stick like a short lance. "Mackenzie, you little bugger!"

David and Pauli jumped back a step, despite the sturdy wire fence separating them from Bishop. Ian placed his hands on his hips, facing the threat, laughing, his skinny chest heaving from his exertions. A trickle of sweat ran through the mud mustache and he wiped it with the back of his hand, spreading the mess in a streak across one cheek so that Hitler disappeared and all that remained was Ian's fuck-you face. "What?"

Bishop could barely speak. He smacked the wire mesh with his stick. "What? *What?* I'll give you bloody what!" He jabbed the stick through the mesh and Ian danced back, laughing.

"Missed!"

David snickered, and Bishop turned on him. He stared at David for a moment before turning and pointing his swagger stick toward the Germans.

"Look at them," he said to David. "They're getting fed, they're getting paid."

David watched the florid face and the mean eyes.

"Do you think your dad's getting the same treatment?"

David blinked but said nothing.

"Do you think they're giving him three squares a day, and beer and smokes? Do you?"

David stared at the red face.

"No, he's not. I'll tell you what he's getting-"

"Fuck you!" Ian jumped at the fence and kicked at Bishop's right hand where it grasped the mesh. Bishop started back.

"Fuck you," Ian said again.

Bishop's mouth twitched. He glanced behind him at the prisoners and the several Veterans Guards watching the show. He turned back to face the boys. "You'll be sorry for this," he said quietly. "Now, I'll advise the three of you to leave. I'll be talking to your parents about this—all of you." His gaze touched Pauli in particular. "It could mean trouble for them."

Pauli nudged Ian. "Come on, Ian. Let's go, eh?" He whispered,

"I'll get shit." The Italian Aiello family—Pauli was only the second generation in Canada—had been the target of nasty comments from some in Willow Creek.

Ian looked at David, who shrugged. "Ah, shit, come on, then," Ian said.

They gathered up their fishing tackle and began a slow withdrawal. David turned once and saw Bishop's gaze on him. He caught a movement beyond Bishop and glanced to where Steve Roper was standing with Joe Kenny. Roper was giving him a thumbs up sign, and nodding his support. David flicked a smile at him, and Roper grinned. David's eyes swept the German ranks and found the sailor's gaze fixed on him. The German's face was creased with the kind of look David's mother got when she was bandaging a cut for him. David thought it was an odd kind of look to get from a German.

- -

The three boys stopped at the crossroads and Ian offered his assessment of Bishop.

"He's an asshole, Davie. Nothing but a big fat asshole."

"Sergeant Major Asshole," an inspired Pauli added. David laughed.

"He's got no business talking about your dad like that," Ian said. "And he knows bugger-all anyway. That's what my mother said, when he came round our place once. She told him to piss off. Then she said he's as dumb as a stump."

David and Pauli punched each other and staggered about as Ian catalogued Bishop's deficiencies.

"Dumb as a stump!" Pauli howled. "A big fat dumb stump!" He fell, laughing, against David until David had to shove him away.

"And she said they don't come any dumber than that!" Ian shouted. The three of them bumped and clung onto each other, shouting with laughter that continued until they reached the dirt road intersection where they went their separate ways.

"See you tomorrow!" Ian shouted.

chapter ten

Kristin Evans stood back from the window in the front room and studied David as he approached the house. His face was set in thought. Questions ahead, she figured. She watched him step over the cracks between the paving stones in the path leading to the front porch. He stopped at the bottom step, pushed a finger into his ear, and poked around the inside, removed the finger, examined it, rubbed whatever he had found between his finger and thumb, and flicked it away. His brow creased and he chewed slowly on his bottom lip. He puckered his mouth, turned his head to the side, and expelled a dollop of frothy spit. He watched the spit land and seemed satisfied with the result.

Kristin was busy straightening a pile of newspapers when he opened the door and entered the room.

"You going to clean those trout?" she asked. "Or am I?"

David's head lifted. He chuckled when he saw the teasing smile.

"Pauli got a tiddler, nothing else, I think it was too hot."

He stopped at the sideboard and picked up the framed picture of his father in uniform, the one the newspaper had borrowed to copy when the news came that Gareth Evans had been taken prisoner.

"I imagine it was." She wondered what was going through his head. He asked the damndest questions sometimes: *"Will they give my dad pyjamas where he is?"* I should think so. *"Will he get cocoa at night?"* I hope so, sweetheart. *"Will they bring him home in a truck when they let him go?"*

Dear God, David.

- -

David wondered if his dad would look the same when he came home, or if he would have changed because he'd been in the war. He remembered back a few weeks when he and his mom went to Lethbridge to see his nana and grandpa. A fellow looked over the fence from the Fraser's house next door and said, "Well, if it isn't young Davie! How's it going, Davie?"

David guessed he was supposed to recognize the man, but he didn't. The man looked sort of sad and turned and trudged back through the open door and into the house. When he asked his mom who the man was, she said, "For heaven's sake, David, that was Rick Fraser! He used to play wheelbarrows with you. You remember, don't you?"

Of course David remembered playing wheelbarrows with Rick Fraser. Rick would make him put his hands flat on the floor, then he would catch David by the ankles and lift him and David would be the wheelbarrow. He remembered how he felt the blood rushing to his head and getting up all red-faced and a bit dizzy after he had wheel-walked the length of the room.

But Rick Fraser didn't look anything like this man. Rick Fraser used to stop in at Grandpa's on his way from high school and was always laughing and tickling David. He had shiny black hair and a red face and a big white smile that David's mother used to say would get Rick into trouble with the girls one day.

The man who called to David across the fence didn't laugh hardly at all and his face was all shiny and stiff-looking on one side and sort of sucked in and folded over on the other, and his hair was more dirty-grey than black and had streaks of white in it.

David said maybe it was another Rick Fraser, but his mom said no, it was the same one but he had been wounded in the war in Africa and had been in hospital for a year. David was sure his dad had not been to Africa. David also heard his mother and his nana say how Rick couldn't even go to the bathroom properly for either a number one or a number two. He asked his mom what they meant, but she just shook her head and started talking about getting him new clothes for starting back at school.

- -

She watched him now as he replaced the photograph on the sideboard. He sat at the table next to the window.

"Mom, do you think grasshoppers feel pain?"

Kristin rolled her eyes, then, "Yeah, I guess they would," she said. "I don't see why they wouldn't. I think it's fish that don't, isn't it?"

David nodded absently.

"We have to get you some new boots while the sales are on," Kristin said. "School in three weeks."

David chuckled. "That's if they find a teacher, right?"

The newspaper said schools in southern Alberta might not open on time because there was a shortage of teachers because of the war. Ian had run around whooping when David reported that news.

"I imagine they'll make a special effort for Willow Creek," Kristin laughed, but David had gone back to gazing out the window, and his knees were swinging together.

Suddenly the leg movements stopped and he shifted in his chair. "We went to see the Jerries."

She was quiet. Her smile was gone. She sighed, "I thought we agreed that—"

"Ian and Pauli wanted to." Just a hint of defiance.

"You know you're not supposed to."

David shrugged. "Yeah, but—"

"You know your grandpa will give me hell if he finds out, you know that, don't you? You know what he says."

David nodded glumly, and recited, in a rich Welsh sing-song, "'The only good German's a dead German, *see*?'"

She turned her face away to hide the laughter that threatened at David's mimicry of his grandfather.

"Is he right?"

Oh, God.

"Is he right, that they're only good after they're dead? What good are they if they're dead?"

"I don't think that's exactly what he means."

"What does he mean, then?"

"I think he means that he thinks all Germans should be dead. That they're not any good when they're alive."

"I thought so."

David glanced at the picture of his dad again. "They don't look much different when you get up close, the Jerries. They look like anybody else, really." It was as much question as statement.

Kristin leaned over him and bent down and cradled his head against her breast. "I suppose they might be when you get right down to it."

"Bishop got mad at us—the sergeant major."

Kristin grimaced. The few times Bishop had stopped for gas he had made her skin crawl the way he looked at her. Not like Steve Roper. She knew exactly where she stood with Roper. But two minutes in Bishop's company and she felt like she needed a bath.

"He said we're too nice to the Jerries—not like them with my dad."

Kristin's mouth tightened. She wondered how he had said it, and figured she could guess. *The bastard.*

"Ian called him an ah, a-hole."

Kristin laughed. "Well, Ian would, wouldn't he? Good for Ian," she added firmly. "He's obviously got some use, after all."

David chuckled.

"Did Bishop hear him?"

David grinned. "No, Ian said that to me and Pauli, after. But he had said plenty to Bishop before that anyway." He rolled his eyes, indicating he was not about to repeat what Ian had said.

Kristin laughed out loud. She was still chuckling when she went out into the kitchen and started filling the tea kettle.

- -

David studied the picture on the sideboard. He wondered what his dad might be doing right then. Maybe he had a garden, like some of the German prisoners had planted out at Camp 10. If it was as hot in Germany as it was in Willow Creek, he would have to water it twice a day. He wondered what kind of stuff his dad was growing in the garden and closed his eyes and began seeing the rows of flowers and vegetables—peas and tomatoes and onions and leeks, lots of leeks, the Welsh always have leeks, see—with the soil dark around them with water from his dad's watering can, and fat drops of water on all the leaves. He frowned, thinking of that, the water on the leaves, but then decided he was fairly sure his dad would remember not to do the watering when the sun was on the plants.

chapter eleven

Jack Bishop shifted his bulk in the beer parlour chair and glowered as he recalled the afternoon's events. He drained his glass and waved to the waiter for a fresh one. He'd had no help from Roper or that fucking waster Kenny; they'd just stood there and watched. Roper should know better. Bishop must remind him. The thought cheered him, as did the familiar onset of well-being fathered by the third glass of cold draft beer. He belched, a rumbling, bubbling release that drifted off among the raised voices and clatter of glasses all around him, then he sighed, satisfied.

He pictured the three kids. They wouldn't be so mouthy after he paid a call on their parents. He was looking forward to it. That Kristin Evans, Christ. His hand drifted down to his crotch. He fondled himself, felt things stirring. She had to be needing it, all on her own. Never know your luck. Especially with a bit of weight to pull. Maybe she would pull *this*. Bishop sniggered. The waiter set down a full glass and picked a dime from the coins on the table.

Bishop swallowed a mouthful of beer and glanced around the packed beer parlour in the Willow Creek Hotel. Allied uniforms speckled the crowd, servicemen from the air-training squadrons stationed at the base east of town. Many of the tunics bore bars of coloured ribbons. That was another thing about Roper, he would never wear the ribbons his records showed he was entitled to, including the Silver Wound Badge they'd given him after Vimy, for Christ's sake. Roper said it was ancient history and best forgotten, that anybody with any sense who had been there would feel the same way about it.

Bishop argued that there were lots of veterans proud to wear their medals. He said that if he had been able to go to the front as he had demanded to, if it hadn't been for his trick knee, the one the doctor had said would have prevented *anybody* from going to the front, he would be only too proud to wear his active service ribbons.

Roper had said he had known lots of lads who would gladly have given their right arms to have had a knee like Bishop's. "In fact some of them did," he'd said.

Bishop thought privately that Roper might be a bit of a Bolshie. But then he reminded himself that as his mother always said, it takes all kinds. His mother had looked him up and down when he came home after the war, in his uniform with the single overseas-service decoration.

"What did they give you that for? What did you do to get that?" And her eyes roamed to the Memorial Cross they had sent to remind her of her other son, James. She had placed the silver medal on its purple ribbon in a glass-fronted display case and hung it above the sideboard in the front room, below the picture of a smiling James in uniform.

The Bishop boys' father had died in a foundry accident three months after Jack Bishop's birth. Their mother had transferred her affection, and her ambitions, to her older son. James became the athlete and scholar destined for great things. His accomplishments in every endeavour cast a shadow too broad for Jack Bishop to step out of. When Bishop returned at the end of the war it was as though his mother expected him not only to overcome his own shortcomings, of which she maintained a ready catalogue, but to fill the immeasurable void created by the loss of his brother. This was an unreasonable expectation made even more impossible by the lustre with which, as the years passed, she gilded James' memory. When her heart finally gave up, she died with the unspoken message that it was not just her heart that had failed her.

These were the thoughts that lived in Bishop's soul. And for their corrosive presence he knew he had the Germans to thank. He could not fathom why people such as Roper and Kenny, both veterans, could spare a civil word for them. Still, as long as Jack Bishop was giving the orders, as long as "The Pope" was making the rules, things would be kept in their proper state. The thought was a comfort.

He drained his beer. As he looked for the waiter, he saw Roper come through the door, wiping his brow, looking around.

Ah, shit, the guy isn't all that bad. Bishop was enjoying the buzz of four beers. He raised his arm and waved. He thought he saw Roper's eye catch the signal, but Roper kept moving. Must have missed it. He half stood and called out over the din, "Steve! Roper! Over here!"

- -

Roper could pretend he hadn't heard above the clatter of conversation, could turn and walk out. He had not come here to get stuck with Bishop in one of his Friday night old-buddy moods. On the other hand, he had told Joe Kenny he would see him in here when Kenny's patrol duty and extracurricular activities were completed. And Roper had a thirst that would scare a camel.

He lifted a hand to acknowledge Bishop, alone at a table by the far wall with an empty glass in front of him, and started threading through the clutter of tables.

Many of the crowded tables were occupied by farmers in for the weekend shopping. The women did the shopping and the farmers drank beer and talked crops and the weather and the war. The men had all gone to school with each other as boys and now farmed within a few miles of Willow Creek. They were in uniform—GWG bib overalls and shirts with sleeves rolled up on working arms dark as varnished oak. Roper marked the scattering of allied uniforms and guessed their numbers would increase before the night was out. Possibly the entertainment would be a punch-up between the Aussies and the Yanks again.

Kenny had said he could be a bit late, that he had some pressing business, which Roper interpreted as Kenny going to get laid. He knew where Kenny was getting it and decided that if the guy wanted to play that close to home, with the risk it entailed, good luck. He resigned himself to spending some time with Bishop, who couldn't have been here too long because Roper had seen him at the camp only an hour before.

Roper had shucked his uniform and changed into slacks and a clean shirt at the house where he and three other guard members, including Joe Kenny, were billeted. Bishop was in uniform. Bishop was always in uniform. Roper often felt that without the uniform the man would be invisible. Sometimes he was tempted to feel sorry for Bishop, for the caricature he had created for himself. The temptation never lasted very long.

Roper squeezed past tables loaded with glasses of beer. He was greeted by farmers who knew him from the delivery of low-priced German labour, and from other, more informal, arrangements.

"Steve." Henry Jensen looked up as Roper eased past the farmer's chair. "I was coming to see you—"

"Taken care of, Henry, no sweat. Next week or so, one choice specimen of the Aryan race coming your way. No extra charge," he added with a grin and a wink.

"Not much anyway," the farmer laughed. "We'll look after you, don't worry." As Roper moved away, Jensen called, "What's his name?"

Roper stopped and thought for a second, then, "Peter Weiss. Nice young feller."

Jensen laughed. "Sounds almost local."

"Probably has family in Winnipeg," Roper said. Jensen and his cronies roared. Jensen wanted to pursue it, but Roper said, "Gotta go, Henry, the Pope's on his throne." He indicated Bishop, who lifted his glass to the farmers.

"Thanks," Roper said as Bishop pointed to fresh glasses a waiter had just delivered.

Roper lifted one and took a long draft. "Ahhhh! That's what was missing." He tipped the glass and finished the rest. "Jesus, that's better."

Bishop looked around and signalled the waiter, a wiry man in his late sixties. "More beer for my corporal!"

The waiter nodded, and shot Roper a sympathetic grin.

Two beers appeared. Roper reached for his pocket, but Bishop had already flipped coins onto the man's tray and waved him away. His treat. Yet it was only a couple of hours before that Bishop had given Roper a don't-mess-with-me glare on the parade square when his expression had shown clear disapproval of Bishop's ranting at the new prisoners.

"Cheers, then, Steve." Bishop raised his glass.

Always tries to make up, away from the camp. He knows he steps over the line with the Germans, but that never stops him from doing it the next time. Almost like he has to do it because somebody's watching, measuring him.

Roper knew a couple of Limey officers like that in the First War, a green, arrogant second-lieutenant, and a snotty chinless wonder of a captain. Both finished up shot dead, neither one of them by the enemy.

"So, you getting much?" Bishop asked. His conversational set-piece.

Roper shook his head, glum. "I think they're rationing it, Jack. I think the government's stockpiling it somewhere."

Bishop sputtered in his beer.

"Warehouses filled with pussy," Roper said. "Going to be a hell of a rush for it when this lot's over."

Bishop's laughter boomed out across the beer parlour, lifting heads and halting conversation. His words were just beginning to slur. That meant soon he would choose one of two directions: stay here and get drunk until closing and somebody pointed him the way home, or down a couple more fast ones and then ask for a ride home. During the ride he would describe in embarrassing detail what he intended to do with Mrs. Bishop when he reached home. Roper was betting on the second routine tonight.

"Gotta take a leak," Bishop said. He stood, signalled the waiter for two more beer, swayed, and steered toward the can.

He returned, bumping into a couple of tables on his way, at the same time Joe Kenny walked in through the far door and looked around, accustoming his eyes to the relative dimness. Roper held a hand up and waved it until Kenny saw it and made his way to the table.

Bishop remained standing and made an exaggerated bow as Kenny arrived, waving Kenny to an empty chair. "Whaddya know there, Joe?"

Buddy time. Jesus.

Kenny examined Bishop. He grinned. "Pecker tracks."

Bishop squinted. "Huh?"

Kenny pointed down to Bishop's pants. "Pecker tracks. You know," and recited, "No matter how much you shake your peg, the last drops always go down your leg."

Recognition bloomed on Bishop's face and he looked down at the dark spots staining the right crotch area of his khaki uniform pants.

"Aw, shit." He rubbed futilely at the stains. He sat down heavily, re-arranged himself, and smiled owlishly at Kenny. "So, are *you* gettin' much, Private Kenny? Ol' Roper here figures the government's rationin' it! Rationin' pussy!" He raised his glass, a salute to Roper's hoarding theory.

"Where do you get the coupons?" Kenny asked, deadpan.

Bishop exploded, coughing and sputtering beer down his shirt and onto the table. "Coupons!" he roared. "Fuckin' coupons! Hey, *'fuckin'* coupons, get it?" He rolled in his chair, banging on the table with the palm of one hand, and sputtering and repeating, "*Fuckin'* coupons!"

Finally, he settled down, laughing as he redirected himself to his beer, swallowing half the contents of another full glass. "Bes' times," he slurred. "Off dudy, tha's the bes' times. Ol' soldiers together. Ol' comrades together. Whaddya say, boys?" He lifted his glass and waved it and the remaining beer slopped dangerously close to the rim.

"Waddya say, hey?" he repeated loudly, and Roper lifted his glass and said, "For sure, Jack," and he and Kenny dutifully clinked glasses with him.

"Ol' comrades," Bishop repeated. Roper and Kenny exchanged looks.

"Goin' home." Bishop stood and straightened his shirt and pants. "Goin' home and get some." He laughed and leaned over to Roper. "Ain' rationed for me, ol' buddy! No coupons for the sergeant major!"

Kenny laughed and slapped the table.

"Gimme a ride," Bishop said to Roper. "You got the Jeep?"

It was about a quarter mile to the house the Veterans Guard had rented for Bishop.

Roper nodded. "Sure," he said. "Be back," he told Kenny.

Bishop swayed during the short ride. He also sang, in a surprisingly pleasing and tuneful baritone, from Vera Lynn's repertoire, including "We'll Meet Again" and "White Cliffs of Dover". Tears of beery sentiment soaked his face by the time Roper stopped the Jeep outside the small two-storey house with the green-painted siding and the yellow front door. Bishop lurched from the Jeep and turned to Roper.

"Friday ni', right?"

"That's right, Jack."

"Know wha' that is?"

"No, what?"

"Nookie night in Canada!" Bishop bellowed, and Roper's laughter was spontaneous as Bishop displayed a triumphant grin.

"Thanks for the ride," Bishop said. "But lissen." He nodded gravely. "'Jack' is okay, you know, in the bar an' that, but—"

"I know. Otherwise it's 'Sergeant Major'. Don't worry, Jack, I know the drill. I'm an old soldier, remember?" He raced the motor and eased the stick into reverse.

"Gotta go, okay?"

"Right," Bishop said. "Okay." Then, "An' we won't forget the other thing either, will we Steve, eh?" He laughed and placed his right forefinger up against the side of his nose and winked repeatedly.

Roper shook his head dutifully. "No, we won't forget that."

Bishop was about to add more, but Roper cut the Jeep back in a short arc, went into a turn with his foot on the pedal, and aimed for the Willow Creek Hotel.

Bishop watched the Jeep retreat. "Damn right we won't forget it, buddy," he mumbled.

- -

Joe Kenny was leaning back, his chair balanced on two legs, smiling at his thoughts, when Roper slid onto an opposite chair and looked across the puddled table.

"You did it again, didn't you? Broad daylight as well."

Kenny laughed. "You're right."

"You're pushing your luck."

Kenny shrugged. "Only comes around once, my friend. Get it while it's going, I figure. An' I'll tell you, I never got a gallop with ol' Alice like I do with this one, God bless her."

"Who—Alice?"

Kenny laughed as he crashed his chair back onto four legs and spilled beer down his shirt front. "Anyway," he said, "what the hell's the matter with you, you jealous?"

Roper shook his head.

"You ain't gettin any, that's your problem," Kenny persisted. "'Less you're payin' for it, them trips to Calgary. Eh? That it? You gettin into them hookers' pants up there? You want to watch that, ol' buddy, things start t' fall off, you not careful." He emptied a glass and plopped it down on the table. "Couple more here!" he yelled over the hubbub.

- -

Helen Bishop glanced up from her ironing board in the kitchen when Bishop pushed through the front door. Her face clouded. She continued pressing the khaki shirt, banishing all creases as demanded by her husband. She drove the blunt point of the heated iron hard into the shirt's breast area, her knuckles bunched and white. She was barefoot in the day's late heat and wore just an aged silk slip under a thin cotton housecoat. The contours of her full, still firm breasts, with their copper-coloured nipples, were silhouetted in the light from the kitchen window against the slight fabric of both garments.

Bishop grunted at the sight. His breath quickened. If it was anything about Helen Smith that had attracted Bishop, apart from her apparently compliant nature, it was her tits, the size and quality of them and the shape and colour of her nipples, large wedges of copper which, when handled, rose into round, pointed peaks. He stood, slightly swaying, his eyes, the wet orbs of the dedicated drinker, fixed on his wife's nipples. He reached out to touch one and she pulled back from his fingers, raising the hot iron like a shield in front of her as she did.

"I'm busy." She resumed work on the khaki shirt, sliding the iron back and forth, rhythmically, on the sleeve. Her housecoat, with the top two buttons missing, fell slightly open as she made each forward stroke, and the silk of her slip rode forward across the heavy, bronzed tips, then back across them with the return stroke.

Bishop's tongue pushed his lips open. He growled, "Let it wait."

She stopped ironing, placed the iron down. She closed her housecoat and folded her arms across her breasts.

"You smell like a brewery," she said.

Bishop's gaze remained fixed on her breasts. "A coupla beer," he shrugged. "'Iss Friday night."

He took a step toward her. His hands came up and touched her arms. For a moment it seemed she might resist. Bishop scowled. She shrugged and lowered her arms and let the housecoat fall open. She closed her eyes and kept them closed while he pulled her to the floor, roughly fingered then sucked and slobbered on her nipples, then spread her legs apart with one meaty hand and directed himself into her with the other. He pumped and grunted for a brief few seconds before finishing his business with a prolonged, shuddering groan. He rolled off her and stumbled to his feet.

She lay still as he reached for a blue flower-patterned white dish towel that hung from a cupboard door knob. He wiped himself with it, dabbing off the final, pearl-like drops from the retreating helmet of his now sagging penis. He crumpled the towel and wiped his florid, sweating forehead, and dropped the towel on her chest.

She searched for an unstained part and wiped herself with it. She got back to her feet and arranged her slip and closed her housecoat around her. She rolled the towel into a ball and dropped it into the sink. She walked past him and into the bathroom, where she turned the shower taps on to their fullest force.

chapter twelve

Kristin Evans glanced up at the sound of the approaching Jeep. She wiped a damp strand of hair away from her forehead and continued sweeping up the thin drifts of dust and bits of dead grass an overnight wind had set down at the base of the gas pump.

The Jeep wheeled in from the road. She let Steve Roper and his passenger wait until she finished. She brushed the sweepings into a tin dust pan and dumped them into a garbage can next to the pump. She leaned the straw broom up against the pump and dusted her hands on her coverall. Only then did she step back and allow Roper to move the Jeep in closer. He applied the hand brake and killed the motor. If her deliberateness had been meant to test Roper's patience, she need not have bothered.

He smiled. "Nice day."

Kristin nodded. "What can I get you?"

"Well, tell you what. I had to go without coffee this morning, We ran out. So, if you had any in stock, you could walk across to the store and I could watch, and that would get my heart started." He laughed and ducked as she made as if to swing at his head with the broom.

Kristin contained an urge to laugh at Roper's bold smile. "You're hopeless, you know that? So, do you want gas, or not?"

"I do want gas. And this is Peter." Roper indicated a German POW in the passenger seat. The blonde-haired young man smiled shyly and said, "Good morning."

Kristin replied with a formal, "Good morning," as she took the gas hose down and placed the nozzle in the Jeep's gas tank.

"I'm taking Peter out to Henry's place," Roper said. "Little extra help for Henry and Martha."

Kristin said, "They'll appreciate that, I'm sure."

Roper glanced across the black-topped semicircle at two cars parked near the shop, a 1934 black Ford and a grey Chevy of the same vintage.

"Getting to be like Picadilly Circus," he said.

"Morgan's here," Kristin replied. "Your old comrade."

Roper laughed, pleased at her tone.

"And Sally Marshall," she said, nodding at the Chevy.

"I'll bet they're both watching," Roper said, and then, as Kristin finished the fill, "Oops, speak of the devil. How do?" he said civilly as Morgan Evans approached across the blacktop, with Sally Marshall a step behind him.

Kristin's father-in-law ignored Roper's greeting. His sour gaze rested on the young German in the Jeep. A scattering of dark blue scars on Morgan Evans' cheeks, the legacy of coal dust wiped unthinkingly along with sweat into cuts and scratches during years of shifts underground, lent a particular menace to his examination.

"Getting chauffeured now, are they?"

Roper sighed, and was pleased to see his own distaste for the man reflected in a flicker in Kristin Evans' eyes.

"It's called taking them to work," Roper said. "He's going to the Jensen's place for a couple of weeks. Right, Peter?" He turned to the POW.

The young man nodded, avoiding Morgan's glare.

Sally Marshall had been chattering at Morgan until they reached the Jeep. Now she directed her flow at Kristin. "I was just saying to Morgan, Kristin, that sometimes they're a real blessing and I don't know what we would do without them. We'll get a couple more before the harvest won't we?" She looked at Roper who, knowing enough to stay silent while Sally's mouth was moving, nodded affirmation.

"They're very good workers, you know," Sally advised Kristin. "And really nice young fellows. When you get to know them, that is." After a pause for breath, she added, "For Germans, I mean. Quite nice, really."

Roper caught Kristin's resigned expression as Sally Marshall prattled on. He raised his blonde eyebrows, and Kristin smiled. Roper handed her the signed gas chit.

In the Jeep, the German POWs glanced at Morgan, who glowered at him.

Kristin spoke to the German, "You'll like it at Henry and Martha's; the Jensens are good people."

The young man's eyes shone at the encouraging tone, while he worked out the message. He smiled, a flash of gratitude. "Thank you," he said.

Roper said quietly, "Attagirl."

Morgan Evans snapped, "Jesus Christ!" and turned a hostile face toward his daughter-in-law.

Kristin looked past Morgan to Sally Marshall. "I've got some Jello under the counter, Sally. I got two cases in."

"I'll take them!" Sally said, and cackled as Kristin said, "You'll take four *packets*, is what you'll take."

"Better than nothing." With attention now on her, Sally was primed. She rattled on. "I need some inner-tube patches. And some glue. Alex forgot them. Men. I tell you, honestly, there's always something, isn't there—always picking up after them, you know? My mother always said you can't live with them and you can't live without them. That's for sure, isn't it?"

Steve Roper was pressed not to laugh, watching Kristin's changing expressions—from irritation to disbelief and finally bemused resignation—as Sally Marshall, barely pausing to breathe, pursued the merits of having a man in the house. The woman was not malicious, Roper thought, just totally self-absorbed, and maybe a little bit dumb.

Kristin remarked as she and Sally walked toward the shop, "You must be good and busy, with this weather and all." It was as though she had wound up a gramophone and set the needle down.

"Oh, you wouldn't believe it! Only time I see Alex these days is at meal times—and bed time, of course! Oh, he's always there then, let me tell you. But work—well, I tell you, Kristin, if we didn't have the Jerries, I don't know how we'd manage. I really don't. Thank God for small mercies, is what I say, eh?"

Kristin appeared to take a deep breath as Sally Marshall stopped talking at the entrance to the store. "I'll get the Jello and stuff," Kristin said.

Roper laughed. "She's a beauty, isn't she?"

There was only Morgan and the German within hearing, and Morgan said, "What? Who?"

"That Marshall woman," Roper said. "Going on about thanking God for the Germans, and about her old man and bed time, on and on with young Kristin there—she's not the sharpest knife in the drawer, is she?"

Morgan Evans' face was livid.

"Know what I mean?" Roper said.

"I know what you mean!" Morgan's quick anger surprised

Roper. "I know bloody well what you mean!" He stepped forward, a hand raised.

"Hey!" Roper stepped back. "Easy," he said. "Now, what's your problem, Morgan?"

"What's my problem, is it?" Morgan snapped. "Aye, well, I'll tell you what the problem is, boy." His roused voice climbed and dipped in the rhythms of the Rhondda Valley. He stabbed a thick, work-hardened finger at Roper. "You bloody stay away from her, that's what the problem is, see? From Kristin. You just stay away from her, see?"

"Hey, I'm a customer," Roper said, careful of Morgan's anger, but not intimidated. "That's all. A customer, okay?"

"Maybe," Morgan retorted. "But not for want of trying, though! Oh, I know your kind, all right. Any woman on her own will do, isn't it? Well, she belongs to my son, that one, and he's away—because of these sods, see!" He stepped close to the Jeep and stabbed a hand toward Peter Weiss, who ducked away from his anger.

Roper grabbed Morgan's raised arm. "Jesus, man, it's nothing to do with him! Look at him, for Christ's sake—he's a kid, that's all, a kid." He released Morgan's arm. "You're getting yourself worked up over nothing. Let it go, okay?"

Morgan glared at Roper. He said nothing, but his hand gradually lowered, and, grudgingly, he stepped back. "You just mind what I said," he growled. He turned and walked toward the shop.

Roper swung himself into the Jeep and started the motor. He smiled at the prisoner. "Fuck him. And the horse he rode in on, right, Peter?"

"Horse?" the young German puzzled.

"Just an old Canadian saying," Roper laughed. He hit the gas pedal and the Jeep bounced out onto the road and raced off, sending up ragged streamers of dust behind it.

Sally Marshall stepped back from the shop doorway as Morgan approached. "I think they had a row. Morgan looks mad as a wet hen."

Kristin dropped the last of Sally's items into a paper bag. "He often is. Here you go, Sally." She handed her the bag. "And don't work old Alex too hard," she added dryly.

"I'll tell him what you said!" Sally shrieked. Kristin laughed as the other woman waddled out the door.

Kristin examined the rows of canned goods on the shelves next to the counter. Some were out of line and she liked them to be neat. She took the folding step ladder from against the shop's back wall and set it up in place in front of the shelves. She was on the third step, re-arranging the cans, when Morgan stomped back into the store. Kristin turned and glanced at him, then resumed her work.

From outside came the sound of Sally Marshall's Chevy starting up, and then the car leaving.

Morgan walked up close to the ladder. Kristin could smell the stale pipe-tobacco miasma he carried with him.

"I watched you," he said.

She turned her head and held his gaze with hers.

"I saw you smiling at him." Each syllable uglier than the one before it.

Kristin sighed. "Don't start with me, Morgan."

"I saw you smirking at each other when she was on about going to bed and that—you can't fool me, I'm not stupid altogether!"

"Shut up, Morgan." She had never talked to him like that, but she had had enough of Morgan Evans.

"I know what's going on!" Morgan snarled. "You're carrying on with him, that's what's going on, isn't it? Aren't you?" His voice was thick, grating.

Kristin flushed. Words climbed into her throat and fought to be released. She forced them back, stayed calm, and resisted the urge to throw her anger back at him.

She said, "'Carrying on'? Are you asking me that, or telling me?"

"I don't have to ask!" Her composure seemed to fan the fire of his rage. "Anybody can see what's happening, can't they? If they're not bloody blind. It's clear as day, isn't it? All that smirking and smiling. When does he come, then? At night, in the bloody dark, is it?"

Kristin's controlled calm grew to a visible contempt as Morgan ranted.

"He would, wouldn't he, his kind? Sneak in, in the dark, get what he wants from somebody else's woman, getting her to do all the stuff for him, and slide out again, the bastard! And you!"

Spittle flecked in the corners of Morgan's mouth as he flung the accusations, and as the accusations became more detailed,

Kristin, not for the first time, wondered about the real motives behind Morgan's outburst. She had the unsettling feeling that this tirade was rooted more in a perverse jealousy than in any concerns for her and her marriage vows to his son. She had seen Morgan furtively watching her when she did small things, like take off her coverall and adjust the light frock she wore under it, or reach up to hang up something in the kitchen, or undo her hair and let it down.

Morgan's chest rose and fell in great panting swells as he continued. "Everybody knows! That Marshall woman knows, you can see it on her face! And my son off in a concentration camp. Slut, that's what you are, and that's what he'll find out when he gets back, I'll make good and sure of that!"

"Get out!"

The words caught him like a smack in the face. He glanced around the store, as if looking for the real source of the order, as if he couldn't believe it had come from Kristin. He raised a hand and wiped a speckle of froth from the corner of his mouth. "What?"

"I said, get out." Kristin's face was drum tight.

"You can't talk to me—hey!" Morgan yelped and ducked as Kristin flung a can of condensed milk that glanced off his shoulder.

"Get out!" She reached for more cans paraded in neat ranks on the shelves behind. "Get out of my shop! Get into your bloody car and go!"

Morgan jumped and yelled at the sharp pain as a can of Heinz beans in tomato sauce bounced off his left elbow. He flung his hands up to deflect a barrage of victual-filled missiles as Kristin abandoned all pretense of rational behaviour.

"Get out of my life!" She jumped down from the ladder and went for him with a can clutched in each raised hand, one of cling peaches in syrup, the other mixed fruit salad.

Morgan fled. He careered through the door and down the shop steps, staring back over his shoulder as he hurried to his Ford sedan.

"You haven't heard the last of this!" He yelled it through the rolled-down side window as he started the motor and pulled onto the road.

Kristin heard her own ragged breathing as she watched Morgan's retreat. She took several deep breaths to steady herself. Her palms were slippery with sweat. She put the two cans she was gripping down on the top step, and braced herself against the door frame. She wiped her hands, brushing them up and down several times against her coverall, ridding herself, it felt, of more than just the accumulated trickle of perspiration.

After a while she picked up the two cans and went inside and placed them on the counter. She walked over to the house and made herself a cup of coffee and smoked two cigarettes while she sipped the coffee and considered what the consequences of her attack on Morgan might be. There was no other witness. She decided that Morgan was unlikely to tell anyone that he called his son's daughter a slut and that she bombarded him with canned fruit and beans. She would deal with it if or when she had to.

She swilled the cup and walked back to the shop. Inside, she examined the scattered cans on the oiled wood floor. She felt a a trembling, a rush of rising laughter. She placed a hand to her mouth, as if to contain it, but the laughter escaped, pushing past her fingers, a burst of full-blown merriment that was like a bird suddenly freed from captivity. It soared on fluttering wings into every crack and crevice in the shop, trilled along every shelf, and danced among the shafts of morning sun that reached in through the open door.

Kristin began re-filling the shelves, humming a couple of bars of a Glenn Miller tune, "In the Mood". She was still tidying up when she heard David. He was whistling and his feet were stomping in time as he marched across the blacktop toward the shop. His tune was "Whistle While You Work." "Old Hitler bought a shirt, Himmler wore it, Goering tore it ..." She smiled at the version that had become popular with small boys who, as their contribution to the war effort, delighted in pouring ridicule on Adolf Hitler and his associates.

David's whistling stopped as he put his head and shoulders in through the doorway. "Hi, Mom."

"Hi, Davie."

'Davie.' Her good-mood name.

"What're you laughing at?"

"Hitler's dwarfs," she replied, and, after a second, David caught on and chuckled with her.

"Where's Grandad? I thought he was staying for supper."

"So did he," Kristin said. "But he remembered he had to do something so he decided he'd better go back."

David said, "Oh." He walked over until he was directly below her. He watched while she replaced the last can of fruit salad. He worked diligently on a loose floorboard with the toe of his scuffed boot.

"Mom?"

"What?"

"Well, you remember you said I could stay over at Ian's some time?"

"I said *maybe*—"

David rushed the rest. "Well, Ian's coming over and we're going over to the Spook House, and Pauli too, and then Ian's mom is going to stop by here to pick him up when she's in town and Ian wanted to know if I could go back with them and stay over there tonight."

She studied his face, the cheeks, tanned and damp with summer perspiration, the deep brown eyes rapt on hers now and filled with hope. She wanted to lean down and take his face in her hands, and kiss it.

Instead, "Hmm ... so Ian wanted to know that, did he?" she teased. "Just Ian?"

David's eyes sparked suddenly, and he chuckled. "Well, and me." He held her smile with his own.

Kristin lifted her hands in mock surrender. "You could talk the robin off a starch box, David Evans. What the heck, why not?"

David's eyes flashed. "Yahoooo! Thanks, Mom! Thanks!" He turned and raced out of the store as Kristin called after him, "David, you get some lunch before you go anywhere, you hear me?"

She heard the screen door slam as David went through the front door into the house. She stepped down from the ladder and stood back to admire the newly sorted rows of canned foodstuffs. That looked much better.

chapter thirteen

Incident at Willow Creek:
The place known as the Spook House is an abandoned farm house that was
frequently visited by the three boys. The approximate location became
known to the German, Kruger, from his conversations with David Evans,
as reported by VGC Cpl. Steve Roper.

Sometimes David just couldn't figure Ian Mackenzie out. Often
he could be really nice, like a few minutes ago when David
announced that he could stay over that night.

"Great, Davie!" Ian yelled. He grabbed David and wrestled
him to the ground, laughing all the time, while Pauli stood and
watched. And Ian was funny. He could fart whenever he wanted to.
He would stick out a finger and say, "Pull that," and when you did,
he would fart, like the finger made it go off. David had tried farting when he didn't have to. He wasn't going to try it again. Then
there were the times when Ian wasn't so nice, or so funny.

Pauli interrupted their fooling around, shouting, "Hey, there's
the Rabbit!"

They got to their feet, brushing grass and dust from their
shirts and pants. Ian had started the wrestling just after they
left the path through the patch of scrub willow and cottonwood
trees and come out into the open grassed area where the Spook
House sat. It was a boarded-up farm house, mostly avoided by
Willow Creek people. Years ago it had belonged to an Irish family, the Dorneys. As the story was told, old man Dorney went
crazy one night and killed the three Dorney kids and his wife
with a shotgun. Then he hanged himself with a bunch of binder
twine from a ceiling beam in the front room. Ian was very good
at pretending to be the old farmer hanging from the beam, his
head twisted over to one side with his eyes squinched up and
his tongue bulging out from a very dead face.

The place had been boarded up for years. Once, Ian forced
open a single board in the back door and stuck his head partway
through the opening, while David and Pauli watched from a comfortable distance.

"Whaaaaagh! He's there!" Ian suddenly screamed as he jumped

back from the door, clutching his throat and bugging his eyes out. David and Pauli yelled and turned and were twenty heart-pounding yards into the bush and going strong when the screams of terror transformed into shrieks of laughter. They returned sheepishly to where Ian lay in the grass laughing and pointing at them.

Even so, David noticed that Ian had not gone beyond the broken board on any of their subsequent visits. They preferred usually to circle the place and speculate on which rooms the killings had happened in, and why somebody, one of the kids, say, hadn't run when the first shots were fired. Ian guessed that the old man had probably fed the whole family Mickey Finns before killing them. Mickey Finns were something to do with powder in whiskey, his new Uncle Wayne from the States had told him, and they knocked people out for hours. His Uncle Wayne also showed Ian a picture of somebody who had been shot in the face in Chicago. Ian's description of the remaining bloody mess had stayed in David's mind for ages.

They also recreated the death of old Dorney, wondering what he had stood on while he fixed the binder twine to the beam and looped it round his neck before kicking away or jumping off the chair or upturned bucket, which were the two most popular choices, before slowly twisting in the air while he choked to death. Ian said his Uncle Wayne told him that people who got hanged like that always shit their pants when they dropped, and he held his nose against the imagined stench.

Ian shouted at the boy they called Rabbit, who had just appeared at the far side of the clearing. "Hey, bunny face—come here!"

The boy was Jimmy Penrice. His family had moved to Willow Creek just after school closed for the summer. The boy was David's age and his dad worked at the airbase where they trained all the pilots. Jimmy had a hare lip, which David's mom had told him was properly called a cleft palate. It was like a big split from the bottom of his nose down to the top of his lips, as if someone had hit him in the mouth with a hatchet and it hadn't healed properly. It made him talk funny, as if he was grunting through his nose, and it showed his two front teeth, which were bigger than normal. David was awfully glad he looked nothing like the kid, who had been nicknamed "Rabbit" the first day he had shown his face in town.

At Ian's shout, the boy looked up and David saw the immediate fear in the face below a head of close-cropped black hair. The boy was carrying a pail of newly picked blackberries.

He tried a quick smile in response to Ian's shout. Ian cackled at the way the smile twisted the boy's mouth, making his face look even more disfigured.

"Come on," Ian said, and sauntered towards the new boy. "Watchagot?" he asked.

Jimmy Penrice shrugged. "Blackberries." Only it came out snuffled, the B sounding fuzzy, which Ian immediately mimicked, making the boy's face redden. Jimmy glanced around, eyes searching for possible escape routes, then back to Ian, who clearly was the most likely source of trouble.

David knew that Ian would use Jimmy's fear. The boy wanted to leave but Ian wasn't about to let him go. This is what David's mom meant when she said Ian liked to play cat and mouse with people. When she said it, David had a picture of Ian patting somebody around with hands that had turned into paws, letting them up for a second, then batting them down again. His mom was right. Ian did it often. Usually, Pauli was the mouse.

"It makes Ian feel better," David's mom said. "If he can put somebody else down, it means he doesn't have to look too closely at himself and the Mackenzie family. There are plenty around like that, you'll find. They're always happiest when the spotlight is on other people's problems, because that means that nobody's looking at theirs."

David thought he knew what his mom meant. Ian wasn't always nasty, but he did like to have somebody he could call names or do things to. This time it was Rabbit's turn.

"I'm going home," the boy said.

Ian was on him, like a terrier on a rat, shoving his face into his and cruelly mimicking his crippled pronunciation. "I'm going home, I'm going home," he snuffled, rattling snot in the back of his throat to get the right sound. Then, as the boy started to move around Ian, Ian grabbed him by the shoulders and dragged him over to the decaying farmhouse and the door with the loosened board. The boy lost his grip on the pail and it went flying as he struggled with the much stronger Ian. Red and black berries scattered across the parched grass.

"What are you doing?" The boy's voice was filled with fear as Ian frog-marched him to the damaged door.

"I'll show you," Ian grunted. He turned to David and Pauli. "Come on and help me," he laughed, as he held the desperately struggling boy up against the door. "This rabbit is trying to run!"

"Hold him," he ordered Pauli, and Pauli took the boy by the shoulder.

Ian glared at David, who hadn't moved. "What's the matter with you, Davie? He's just a fucking rabbit face." He turned and attacked the door, forcing two of the boards until he'd opened a narrow entrance into the old house.

Ian bundled Jimmy's skinny frame through the gap, then grabbed the boards and jammed them together. He hooted as he pushed them shut, closing the day off from the dank darkness inside the Dorney ghost house.

"Now the spooks'll get you, Rabbit! That's old Dorney hangin' up behind you. *Whoooooooooo!*"

David had no idea whether the Penrice boy knew the Dorney story, but there was no doubt about the fear in the voice that came back at them from behind the damaged door, as the imprisoned boy pounded on the wooden boards and begged them to let him out.

"I'm scared! I can't see! Let me out! Please!" The words jammed and fought their way out past his twisted lips and emerged in a rush of injured syllables that had Ian almost falling down laughing as he attempted to imitate them.

"Pleeeease, let me out!" the boy cried.

David imagined the inside. Dark rooms where people had been shot by a father gone mad, their blood spattered against the walls and on the floors. The binder twine in a death loop hanging from a beam.

"Let him out, Ian," David said, running to the door. "Come on, let him out." He pulled against the two split boards.

The shouting inside quieted, but the boy's quick, fractured breathing was still audible from behind the door.

"Hey!" Ian pushed at David with one hand while holding onto the door with the other. "It's a joke, Davie, is all!" He held David off and turned back to the door and shouted, "There's dead people in there, Rabbit! And blood on everything, and fucking ghosts coming to get you!" He laughed his high-pitched laugh.

"Let me out!"

David heard awful fear in the voice. "Let him out, Ian!"

Ian laughed and pushed David away.

"I said, let him out!" He drove his slight body into Ian's mid-section so that Ian fell away from the door and sprawled on the grass, still laughing.

The door creaked open as the Penrice boy realized that the pressure was off it. He scrabbled to open the boards and catapulted through the opening. The boy stood panting and shaking, his stance reminding David of a prairie antelope that he and his dad got close to once. The animal had sensed their presence and stood, quivering, every nerve and muscle prepared for the series of bounds with which it would take its sudden, elegant flight. That's how his dad described it, in something he wrote. But this boy was not elegant as he stood, shaking, looking at his overturned berry pail and its scattered contents.

Ian suddenly came up on one elbow and pointed at the boy. "Pissy pants!" he howled. "Pissy pants!"

David followed Ian's pointing finger. Sure enough, Jimmy Penrice had peed his pants, the proof a dark stain around the crotch of his patched grey flannels.

The boy looked down. He touched the area and pulled his hand back quickly, as though he had been burned. His mouth quivered and he fought back tears. He backed away from Ian, as if distance would diminish his shame. His retreat just made Ian laugh the louder.

The boy's shoe touched his berry pail and he reached down and picked up the empty container. Gripping it tightly, he suddenly bolted, stepping on his scattered berries as he ran.

David felt like running after the kid and telling him not to worry, telling him that Ian was just being stupid, just being an asshole. But the boy was gone.

Ian rolled around on the grass. "Did you see that?" he laughed. "What a pansy, eh? Pissed his pants then ran like a rabbit!"

David stood over Ian, looking down at him. David's fists were clenched. "You do it," he said.

Ian looked up. His face was streaked with tears from laughing. "What?"

David leaned his face closer to Ian. "I said, you do it." He pointed to the Spook House and the door with the two sagging boards. "You go in there and we'll shut the boards up and hold the door closed so that you can't get out. I dare you."

"Ah, shit, Davie, it was a joke. Can't you take a joke?" He looked doubtfully at David as he said it.

"I dare you."

Pauli watched, mouth agape. Nobody dared Ian. Nobody ever had to. Ian was always the one daring everybody else to do the things he did, and most of the time nobody would. Ian was the one who climbed the drain pipe at the Manning house where Miss Wilkinson, the teacher, had a room, and watched her undress.

"She's got little titties but a great big bush," Ian reported, demonstrating with his hands the location and expanse of the luxurious growth. Then he invited the others to repeat his route and confirm the picture. Nobody did, as Ian knew they wouldn't. Pauli wondered if Ian truly had seen Miss Wilkinson's titties, or even if Miss Wilkinson was in the room. He never mentioned his doubts to Ian.

David held his ground as Ian got to his feet. Ian looked down at David from his greater height and sneered, "Are you on his side? Are you on the Rabbit's side?"

David was rattled. Ian had suddenly changed the rules, placed him in Jimmy Penrice's camp and questioned his loyalty.

"I didn't say that. I said, I meant, that you wouldn't like it if somebody did that to you, and I said I dare you to go in there. On your own," he added, recovering some ground.

Ian laughed and suddenly grabbed David's nose and gave it a gentle twist. "Ah, anybody can do that. Watch."

He marched up to the door, pushed back one of the damaged boards, stuck his head partly inside, and shouted, "Helloooo, this is Ian. Who are yoooooou?" He withdrew his head and spun around with his eyes crossed and doing his dead Dorney impression, which drew the usual instant guffaws from Pauli and, eventually, a chuckle from David.

"But you didn't go in," David said, when Ian had resumed being himself.

"Aw," Ian shrugged, and he grinned. "Hey, what're we gonna do at my place tonight?"

The Rabbit was history. The afternoon lay before them. Ian's mother was due to pick them up, a bit before supper time, at David's place.

"What're we gonna do now?" Pauli said, as they wandered away, putting distance between themselves and the Spook House.

David wished they had brought fishing gear. "I dunno," he said. "What do you want to do?"

Ian ran a few steps and launched himself into a cartwheel. He landed lightly on his feet. He rubbed his hands against his pants and grinned. "Let's go see the Jerries."

Pauli looked doubtful. "What if Bishop's there?"

"Sergeant Major Asshole, you mean," Ian corrected him, and the three of them hooted.

"What d'y say, Davie?" Ian said slyly, and David was aware the dare had been turned on him. They watched for his response.

David considered. He knew his mom didn't want him going, not really. But she also hadn't finished up nearly as mad as he thought she would when he told her about the other day, and about Sergeant Major Asshole. And something told him that having just successfully faced Ian down, now was not a good time to back away.

He shrugged. "Sure. Okay."

- -

Sweating and panting, they slowed from a trot and advanced toward the crest of the hill overlooking Camp 10. Ian led the way and directed their movements with hand signals, like the platoon leaders did in the war movies just before they dropped to the ground with machine guns and started mowing down Germans.

Nobody seemed to be doing much inside the wire. The Germans lounged around in groups and David noticed the one in the sailor uniform sitting up against a low pile of lumber near the unfinished foundation of a new barracks hut, talking and laughing with another, younger prisoner. The sailor was whittling away at something with what seemed to be a jackknife. David wondered if they were supposed to have knives and stuff. He wondered if his dad was allowed to have a knife, and thought he would probably need one to eat his dinner with, unless the Germans gave them knives at mealtimes and then took them back, maybe.

His thoughts were interrupted when Ian grunted and pointed to where Bishop had stepped into view from behind one of the barracks huts and was examining the groups of prisoners. The sun bounced off Bishop's cap badge. His swagger stick rested in its usual place under his left arm.

- -

Eric Kruger had noticed the movement at the top of the hill outside the fence. He hid a smile as he caught sight of Bishop starting his rounds. The boys were not supposed to be there, but boys would always do things they were not supposed to do, and they were out of Bishop's physical reach anyway.

He put a careful final touch with his jackknife to the whistle he had carved from a willow twig. He tested it with a soft blow and carefully put the whistle away in his shirt pocket. He felt Bishop's eyes on him and casually allowed his own attention to drift away to other points. Bishop wore the face he reserved for appearances when patrolling within the wire: a fusion of part sneer, part threatening scowl.

- -

"Bishop looks mad," Pauli said as he squinted down into the compound.

"Very mad," David said.

Ian said, "My mother says he looks like that maybe because he's not getting any."

"Not getting any what?" David asked.

Ian shook his head, puzzling. "I'm not sure. I just heard her. She was talking to Mrs. Grant in the bakery and she said, 'Could be he's not getting any, and that's his problem.'"

"Why didn't you ask her?" Pauli said.

"I did, but they just laughed."

Ian said suddenly, "Hey, let's do Goe-balls for them!"

Pauli said, "What, here?" and David rolled over in the grass and covered his mouth with his hands as he laughed.

"Come on!" Ian said. He jumped to his feet and started marching along the hill's crest. As he went he sang loudly to the tune of the Colonel Bogey March:

"Hitler has only got one ball, Goering has two-oo ve-ry small, Himmler is very simmler ..."

Pauli and David joined him in the stanza's last, satisfying, demeaning line: "But poor old Goe-balls has no balls at-aa-aa-allll!"

The words floated down into the compound and the Germans laughed, though more at the sight of the marching boys than any comprehension of the words.

Beside Bishop, Joe Kenny failed to smother a laugh as Ian rounded off the performance with an exaggerated bow. A spattering of applause came from several Germans.

Bishop's scowling attention on the boys was distracted as he noticed the German submarine officer, Kruger, the one he'd heard Roper calling Eric.

Eric? Roper would get charged with fraternization if he didn't back off from that shit. Fraternization added to quite a bit more if Roper wasn't careful. He had Roper's game tagged, all right. And that Kenny. That fucker was hiding something as well.

The German moved his hand in a small waving motion and Bishop followed the direction of the sailor's attention—the bloody Evans kid. Bishop saw that the boy had noticed the German's attention and was watching him with interest.

"Look at that," Bishop said, using Kenny as his audience. "That Evans kid, from the gas station."

Kenny nodded.

"You have to wonder what goes through his head," Bishop continued. "I mean, when you think of the shit his old man must be getting from the Jerries?"

Kenny said, "Yeah, for sure."

"Them stalags ain't cushy spots like these, you know. Slave labour camps is more like it."

Kenny thought he detected approval in Bishop's tone. He was sure of it when Bishop said, "The Krauts know how to run a prison camp. They know how to handle prisoners, let me tell you." As if drawing from some deep well of privileged information, and possibly, it was intimated, from personal experience, which Kenny knew was a large crock of shit, but which opinion he withheld.

"He bothers me, that kid," Bishop mused. "In fact, you know," and a cunning smile split his beefy face, "I might have to go and have a word with his mother about all this."

He leered. "You know her?"

Kenny nodded. "Seen her, Sarn't Major."

Bishop snorted. "That's what I mean! Them tits! Out to here!" He cupped sausage-fingered hands at his chest.

Kenny chuckled dutifully, and inwardly mocked the thought of Bishop ever getting close to a woman like Kristin Evans.

While Bishop talked, the boys had slid quietly down the hill and now stood just a few feet back from the wire.

Eric Kruger watched them inch their way close. "Good afternoon, boys."

Ian had enjoyed the attention they got performing "Goe-balls." "Hiya," he said, and the three boys exchanged grins.

Several prisoners responded with delighted calls of "Hiya!"

The collective greeting roused Bishop from his fantasies of Kristin Evans. "Shit!" he snapped. He marched toward the area of suddenly opened communications between the boys and the prisoners.

It seemed to David that Bishop got bigger and angrier with each approaching step. Beside him Pauli started making his humming sound, "Hmmmmmm, hmmmmm," which he did whenever he got nervous, without knowing he was doing it. He heard Ian muttering, "Asshole," and laughing to himself.

Bishop stopped just a few paces from the wire and swished the air with his swagger stick. Pauli started edging backwards up the hill but David and Ian stood tight.

Bishop was livid but he was not about to get caught again shouting ineffectually through the wire fence while the little bastards thumbed their noses at him. And there were easier targets. He was within a couple of steps of Eric Kruger, who remained sitting passively against the stack of lumber. The smile that the boys had brought to the German's face was gone now, replaced by a carefully neutral mask.

Bishop stared down at the German, tapping the toe of one large highly polished boot against the packed earth.

The German reluctantly raised his eyes to Bishop's face, then lowered his gaze. He glanced sideways at the young pilot prisoner who had earlier caught Bishop's unfavourable attention. 'Be careful,' his unspoken message warned across the short space between them. The pilot looked away, through the wire at the three boys.

- -

David thought it was like being at the movies, waiting to see what would happen next. Something was going to, you just knew. Pauli had stopped near the top of the hill and sat, watching. Beside David, Ian leaned in toward the wire.

Bishop started it. To Eric Kruger he said, "Well, Admiral, hands across the sea now, is it?"

The German's brow creased. After a moment, reluctantly, he turned his head and looked up at Bishop. Other Germans watched from lowered eyes, ready to shift their focus if Bishop looked their way.

Joe Kenny watched nervously.

The German said, "Pardon?"

Bishop glowered. *"Pardon?"* he mimicked. Then, "I said, peace and goodwill is it, now that you can't do any more damage?"

The German appeared to decide the less said, the better. He looked away from Bishop, but that was not going to divert the sergeant major.

"Or—just a minute." Bishop stroked his chin, a thinking man. And it came to him. "Could it be? Yes, it's the little boys that we like. That's it—Hitler's navy likes little bum boys. Bunch of shirt lifters, Fritz, eh? Backdoor artists." He laughed.

Joe Kenny groaned quietly.

- -

Outside the wire, David's brow creased as he puzzled over Bishop's words. But Ian had no problem understanding. Ian snorted, and with the back of his hand wiped his nose. To David's puzzled face, he explained: "Homos."

David laughed uncertainly. Ian had told him and Pauli one day in the willow woods behind the Spook House about one of his visiting air force "uncles". He had asked Ian to help him find a watch he said he had dropped in the bedroom. Ian's mother was out. The airman had just got out of bed and was still half dressed, with only his shirt on, Ian said, and when they were both on the rug and looking under the bed he grabbed Ian and started tickling him and they started wrestling and rolling around, until he had Ian pinned down beside him. Then he took Ian's hand and held it between his legs.

"His dick was like this," Ian told them, using his hands to depict an organ of unlikely length and thickness.

The airman then told Ian to rub it, and Ian described how he was instructed to stroke it up and down.

"Like this," Ian said as he began to rub his own penis. It grew in size as he rubbed it, getting thicker and longer. Suddenly he turned to Pauli and, his breathing ragged, said, "Come on, Pauli, we'll show Davie." Pauli tried to back away as Ian pulled at his pants. "Kneel down! Kneel down!" Ian shouted. He managed to drag Pauli's pants down past his chubby knees while Pauli toppled over, trying to pull them back up. Ian then pressed his penis up against Pauli's bum and pushed back and forth while Pauli scrambled to get away.

David stared at the scene, trying to make sense out of what Ian was doing. He knew about hard-ons, and he guessed that was what Ian had now.

Pauli finally managed to struggle free and dragged his pants up to where they belonged. His face was red, his mouth quivering. "That's what he tried to do to me," Ian said. "He was a homo. They do your bum."

David didn't believe it about the German sailor.

- -

Eric Kruger barely contained his first surge of anger when he realized what Bishop was saying, and he reacted. "That is not the way—"

But Bishop cut him short. "Shut up!"

Bishop glared down at the German. Then, deliberately, he collected saliva around his tongue. He pursed his mouth and spat a frothy gob down toward the German's feet. Some of the spittle flew from the corner of his mouth and hit the German's shirt sleeve.

Eric Kruger examined the result. He took a sliver of wood and brushed the wet spots off his sleeve. "There is no reason to do that."

The restrained objection and the truth behind it seemed to incite Bishop more than retaliation might have done. He bent his bulk over the German. His cheeks bulged, his face turned crimson.

"Don't you bloody well tell me what there's reason for!"

Eric Kruger suddenly was on his feet. The movement was smooth and quick, but careful. Though the sailor had made no move toward him, Bishop retreated a step.

"Hah!" Outside the wire, Ian had read the coward in Bishop's move.

Bishop's lips compressed and he turned his red face and his glare on the boys.

Eric Kruger said, "I am not dirt, to be spit on, Sergeant Major."

Joe Kenny winced and shook his head.

Bishop returned his stare to the German.

Eric Kruger continued. "I did not make this war." Quiet, but loud enough for nearby prisoners, Joe Kenny, and the three boys to hear.

"We did not make the war." He encompassed with an arm the rest of his fellow POWs. "Any more than you did." He nodded at Bishop and at Joe Kenny in turn. "It was made by madmen, by Hitler and people like him."

Outside the wire Ian said, "Holy shit." Beside him, David nodded. A German just called Hitler a madman.

And Eric Kruger was not finished.

Nor was Bishop trying to stop him now. In fact Bishop had folded his arms and a slight smile creased his face.

As a former employer had once said of Bishop, the faster he digs, the deeper he sinks. Bishop let the German dig.

"We do not wish to be here. We wish to be home, with our wives and our children. We are no different from you."

Through the wire, David saw Bishop's mouth twitch at this, and again he thought that the German, who was being very brave, was going to be in trouble if he kept on talking, which he did. David hadn't thought of Germans being brave.

"Except, as you know, we are losing the war. Probably we have lost it."

The sailor turned and pointed to David and Ian, and Pauli, who was working his way cautiously back down the hill.

"I have a son." He nodded to the other prisoners. "Many of these men have children—*had* children, maybe."

David noticed Joe Kenny nodding as the sailor spoke.

"We do not know what will be left." He stopped and shrugged, and the shrug was the cue for Bishop, to whom all eyes now moved.

Anyone not familiar with Bishop might have taken the slow nodding of his head to be a gesture of sympathy, even conciliation, rather than a sly parody of those decent feelings.

Bishop said, "Well now, that's heart-breakin', that is. Heart-breakin'. Isn't it?" He appealed to Kenny, who let the rhetorical question slide past him while he wondered where Bishop was heading. Nowhere pleasant, for sure.

The three boys stepped closer to the wire.

"Same as us, you say?" And louder: "Same as us?" Bishop's mouth opened, closed, and, "You bastard!"

The three boys jumped.

"Fire-bombs on London! Fire-bombs on Coventry!" Bishop's eyes glared.

He jabbed a thick finger at the German's face. "Women and little kiddies burned to cinders! Same as us, you say? You Nazi cocksucker!"

Outside the wire, David held his breath as the German sailor not only stood his ground, but fought back, telling Bishop, "No one has a ... " he struggled for the word and found it "...monopoly on slaughter, Sergeant Major."

For a moment David saw the German as the brave Horatius in the poem that Miss Wilkinson had made them learn by heart and then had David recite for the class, *Horatius:*

Then whirling up his broadsword / With both hands to the height / He rushed against Horatius / And smote with all his might / With shield and blade Horatius / Right deftly turned the blow / The blow, though turned, came yet too nigh / It missed his helm, but gashed his thigh ...

"Do you know about Munich?" the German went on. "Do you know about the women and children there? They are also—"

"Shut up!" Bishop raised his swagger stick.

The German refused to move. "It is the same," he said.

"Shut up!" Bishop slashed at the German's head with his swagger stick. Eric Kruger ducked the blow, grabbed the stick, and tore it from Bishop's grasp.

"Oh, shit!" Ian said.

David gasped.

The German dropped the swagger stick in the dirt. He lowered his hands to his side and stood, feet apart, and waited.

Bishop seemed not to know what to do. His arm was raised, as if frozen in place. His face registered disbelief. Then his arm dropped and his face changed. His eyes narrowed, his mouth tightened. He swung around, took three quick steps across the ground between himself and Joe Kenny. Before Kenny realized his intent, Bishop grabbed the guard's .303 Lee Enfield rifle and spun back toward the German, working the bolt as he did so and ramming a cartridge into the chamber. He lifted the rifle and aimed it. The muzzle sat two feet from and level with the sailor's chest.

A silence clutched the camp, disturbed only by Joe Kenny's scared and whispered, "Jesus Christ!" and a terrified and excited "Oh, *shit!*" from Ian. Pauli, who had made it all the way back down to the wire, grabbed David's hand, then dropped it as David stepped right up to the wire and pressed his face against the rough strands.

David watched the scene as if it was happening in slow motion. He saw Bishop's face, mouth clamped tight, eyes blinking and blazing. He saw the German's face, taut, pale, afraid.

Eric Kruger's hands and arms moved slowly; first out from his sides, then rising, an inch at a time, the palms open and facing upward. The rifle muzzle rose in concert with the prisoner's arms. The German's hands stopped at face level and his palms faced Bishop. The rifle's ascent stopped also, its muzzle now pointed into the German's face, at the bridge of his nose, between the brown eyes filled with the knowledge that at any moment the muzzle could explode into a blast of flame and lead that would turn his head into ...

Like what was left of the gopher's head, with the bloody string dangling with a tooth at the end of it. David watched Bishop's right hand, its forefinger curved around the trigger. A fat bead of sweat broke on Bishop's brow and he blinked as the saltiness trickled down into his left eye. His finger tightened on the trigger.

David's heart pumped, pounding in his chest, sounding like drums in his ears, as he watched Bishop's finger beginning to squeeze the trigger ... don't pull it ... squeeze it.

David screamed. "No! No!" He grabbed the wire fence and spread himself against it, and screamed again, "No-o-o-o-o!"

There was a nanosecond when everything, everyone, froze. Then, slowly, the fragments moved. First the rifle wavered. Then the butt slipped from Bishop's shoulders. It slid gradually down the front of his shirt and trousers, caught briefly on his webbing belt, and finally bumped and rested on the ground with the muzzle pointing to the sky. Bishop looked down at the gun. He frowned, as if wondering how it had arrived there. He lifted a hand and wiped a small tide of sweat from his forehead. He flicked the moisture away so that it formed a scattered rank of tiny craters in the dust around his feet.

The German released a long, ragged breath. His head sagged almost down to his chest, as if the effort to hold it up was too much, and his shoulders slumped.

"His legs are shaking," Ian said from behind David, and David saw that the German's legs really were trembling under the material of his trousers.

"Sarn't Major?" Joe Kenny was beside Bishop. He indicated the rifle, which Bishop still held at a sloppy slope-arms position. Bishop stared at Kenny, then looked down at the rifle, as if still pondering its origins. Slowly, he handed it to Kenny, who stepped away several paces, ejecting the live cartridge as he did.

The German stepped shakily to the stack of lumber. He put his hands out like a blind man and touched the top boards before lowering himself to a sitting position.

Bishop watched, detached, as the German moved away, then he turned abruptly and marched toward the orderly room at the far end of the camp.

Joe Kenny breathed, "Jesus Christ."

Outside the wire, Ian punched David on the shoulder. "Holy shit, Davie," he said, clearly admiring, and then, "Wow, look at that!" He pointed to David's hands where the imprints of the fence wire were deep and red across the palms.

"You stopped him, Davie!" Pauli bubbled.

Ian shoved Pauli aside. "That's what I said, you goof."

Joe Kenny faced them from inside the wire. "Right, lads, I think that's enough for one day, eh? You three take off, now."

Ian looked at David.

Kenny said, "You don't want to crank him up again, do you?" He jerked his thumb after the departed Bishop.

Ian shook his head.

Kenny said, "Good lads," as they started back up the hill.

- -

"He can't keep on treating them like that," Joe Kenny said later to Steve Roper.

Roper shrugged. "The guy's a jerk."

"He's more than that," Kenny said. "He's fucking nuts. He's dangerous, in fact. What about the Geneva Convention? Prisoners are supposed to be treated no worse than—"

"The detaining power's own garrison troops." Roper completed the sentence for him. "I know, Joe, I went to all the lectures."

"Right, so these guys have a right to appeal this kind of shit. We could be witnesses."

"Joe, the Geneva Convention is a nice idea, if it worked everywhere. It doesn't. Check with Herr Hitler on that. And right here, we have Bishop's rules and soon Bishop will get bored and think of something else to occupy that space he calls his mind—"

"In a pig's ass he will. He'll keep after Kruger. You know what he's like. You're the next senior NCO, you could have him by the balls—"

"Forget it, Joe! Forget this witness shit. It'll blow over and nobody'll be any the worse for it. Kruger's tough, and smart. He can handle it."

Kenny persisted. "But they'd listen to you in Lethbridge. They'd have to."

Roper stared at Kenny. "First, if Lethbridge got involved they're more likely to just ship Kruger back there and let him deal with that crowd than do anything about Bishop, who is one of *them*, after all. They're the ones who promoted him. They won't want to look responsible for a fuck-up. You know how these things work. And anyway, I can assure you that the last thing Kruger wants is to be shipped back to Lethbridge. So *nobody* is reporting *anybody*. Got it?"

Kenny opened his mouth to reply, but Roper raised a hand. "Nobody—*Private* Kenny. That understood?"

Kenny frowned, then, "All right. Jesus, I just thought—"

"Don't think, Joe. This is the army."

Kenny shrugged. "Sure. Whatever you say, *Corporal*." He grinned. "Hey, it's no skin off my ass."

"And of course, Private Kenny had no special reason to want to see the Sergeant Major dipped in the shit bucket, did he?"

"Absolutely not, Corporal."

"Good. Let it be, Joe. Just let it be."

chapter fourteen

Kristin sat on the top step and watched the two-seater MG sports car turn sharply off the road and skid to a slanting stop. She laughed when Moira Mackenzie threw a leg over the side of the open car and hoisted herself out without bothering to open the door. The action caused Moira's pale-blue linen frock to ride up her thighs, past the tops of her sheer silk stockings, and expose a tiny pair of scarlet panties not from any store within a long way from Willow Creek. A turquoise silk scarf loosely covered her head of flame-red hair.

Moira's arrival was followed a few minutes later by that of the three boys, who trotted in, sweating and parched and falling over each other to get at the bottles of Orange Crush Kristin set out for them.

Moira was the only woman Kristin had ever known who whenever she was in the mood went without a brassiere and didn't care a fig who noticed. And anyone would notice, Kristin chuckled, recognizing that Moira was in her carefree mood today. She tried to keep a straight face as Moira jiggled across the blacktop toward her, her breasts riding high under the lightweight summer frock.

"Kristin! How you doing?" Moira enveloped her in a hug and a cloud of perfume that evoked wild roses and honeysuckle, squeezed her mightily, and kissed her on the cheek. "I haven't seen you for weeks. I've been tied up, to coin a phrase!" She tossed her blazing mane of hair and sent a shout of laughter into the hot, still air.

"Ooops!" Moira exclaimed, as she caught sight of the three boys peering out from inside the store. "Hi, guys, go and play for a bit, okay?" The three faces withdrew. She pulled a packet of Players from a pocket of her dress and offered them to Kristin, who was still chuckling over Moira's arrival.

You might have some reservations about the Mackenzies generally, Kristin thought, *but you couldn't help enjoying Moira.*

She took a cigarette and accepted a light from an expensive looking silver-coloured lighter. The lighter and the MG, Kristin knew, were both expressions of appreciation from Moira's current lodger, a flight-lieutenant in the Royal Australian Air Force, whom Moira had introduced once as they stopped for gas as "John Gales. Big John. And I mean *big* John!"

Kristin inhaled and blew out a stream of smoke. "It's good to see you," she told Moira. "Nice change from the same old faces." She turned her head toward the shop door. "I don't know if David and Ian have cooked this up themselves, or—"

"No, no," Moira interrupted. "I told Ian to ask David if he wanted to come and stay over." She laughed, "He's such a pain in the ass when he's on his own sometimes, so there's a bit of self-interest involved." She looked hesitantly at Kristin. "Is it all right? I mean, he'll be fine with us. I know some people think ..."

"Of course it's all right," Kristin said quickly. "I know he'll be fine." She caught the flicker of gratitude in Moira's eyes. "It'll give me a break as well," Kristin added.

Moira said, "Right, I'll get them aboard."

Kristin chuckled as Moira stuck her head inside the doorway and groaned, "Oh, Christ, you're here as well, Pauli? Well, what the hell, they do it with sardines—come on, the three of you." The boys headed whooping for the MG and crammed into the passenger seat.

"I'll go slow," Moira said. Kristin nodded and waved at David as Moira crept the sports car out onto the road and pointed it in the direction of the Mackenzie place, about a mile the other side of Willow Creek. Kristin was sure there'd be a stop to pick up a block of ice cream and no doubt a Coke each, at the drugstore.

She went into the store. She took the cash out of the till and dropped it into the empty Maxwell House coffee tin that she would later take into the house. She picked up a fountain pen and a lined paper pad with a page half-filled with writing, much of it scratched out and corrected. She picked out a bottle of Orange Crush and returned to the outside where she sat on the top step, sipping the sweet fizzy drink, the writing pad balanced on her knees. She had finished the cigarette Moira had given her. She lit one of her own and leaned back, putting her face in the shade of the roof's slight overhang. She stared down at the writing pad: "My Dearest Gareth ... " it began. There were a few sentences, but they were mostly crossed out.

She inhaled and slowly blew out a plume of smoke. She tried to blow a smoke ring, but the thing she produced wobbled, drifted away and lost itself in the heat. She pushed her hair back. She had thought she saw a grey hair this morning, but on closer inspection it had turned out to be flecks of face powder. Still ...

An image of Morgan Evans' face rose, uninvited. She tried to push him from her thoughts. Morgan and Sally Marshall. They both had her labelled and parcelled out. She laughed suddenly, choking on the cigarette smoke, as Moira Mackenzie's face supplanted both of them. She could hear Moira's laughing voice saying, "Fuck 'em, Kristin."

Normally, she would have closed the shop up twenty minutes ago, but today there was no rush. For once she could just boil an egg for supper, and maybe a slice of toast with it. It was pleasant for a change to have only herself to do for.

She peered down the road to the south, first hearing the sound then recognizing the shape of the army Jeep, and the posture of the driver behind the wheel. She rose, as if to go inside, then shrugged and returned to her place on the step. She flicked the ash off her cigarette and watched it drop and settle on the worn steps. She concentrated on the letter she had been trying to compose for the past two days.

– –

Steve Roper was satisfied with his day's work. He had delivered the young prisoner, Peter Weiss, to Henry and Martha Jensen, and they had seemed pleased. Martha had surprised the hell out of the kid by placing her considerable arms around him, welcoming him to the farm with an extended hug against her pillow-like bosom. Peter had surfaced looking a little embarrassed, but otherwise quite happy, Roper noted. And proof of Henry's satisfaction with the deal lay in the two bottles of good rye whiskey wrapped in a burlap bag and shoved under the Jeep's driver's seat. There had been a brief discussion of various other business dealings to be conducted in the immediate future, and an unspoken confirmation that loose lips sink ships, so to speak.

Driving back along the narrow, unpaved roads from the Jensen farm, Roper had recalled the other war, when he had, without scruple, lined up young men—boys—like Peter Weiss, in the sights of his machine gun, and watched the heavy slugs chew and chop them into bloodied pieces as they attempted to cross the corrupted few yards of French countryside designated as no-man's land. The boundaries changed by the day, by the hour, in the turmoil of human destruction that had been described as the war to end all wars.

The army, offering $1.10 a day and everything found, had seemed like a grand opportunity to a boy with Steve Roper's history and his circumstances.

Roper was born just south of London, England, to a seventeen-year-old girl whose married lover walked away from her when she became pregnant. She died giving birth and the baby was taken in by the mother's much older unmarried sister. When the baby grew into a lively boy with too strong a head for a middle-aged spinster to handle, young Steve Roper was shipped off to Canada with a boatload of children in similar predicaments. Until he was sixteen he survived as an unpaid and ill-treated servant and labourer on a succession of farms from Ontario to Alberta. At his last "home", in the Peace River country, the farmer had caught Roper in the hayloft with his fourteen-year-old daughter, the girl giggling with her skirts up around her neck and Roper halfway finished one of the rides he'd been giving her almost daily for the past three months. He had concluded that if he wasn't going to get money for his sixteen-hour days, the fucking would be his compensation. It was Roper's good fortune that the farmer was carrying only a wood-tined hay rake when he discovered the joyous carnal activities, and not his shotgun. As it was, Roper quickly headed down the long and lonely road south bearing three parallel jagged and bloody lines on his arse, the scars of which would always be a reminder of his last moment with the dark-haired farm girl. He fled with nothing but the work clothes and boots that were his regular daily attire. But seeing as he had arrived at the farm in much the same condition, he concluded that he had come out about even from the experience. Or if the hay loft activities had counted for anything, maybe ahead some. In Edmonton he saw the posters for the army, and he had no trouble adding two years to his age and getting past the Scottish recruiting-sergeant's desk.

Roper was trained as a machine gunner in Quebec and then in England. His unit, the First Battalion, Canadian Machine Gun Corps, was part of the Canadian Corps that was ordered to take Vimy Ridge, a key link between the Germans' new Hindenburg line and their main trenches near Arras, on Easter Monday 1917, four months past Roper's seventeenth birthday. The Germans had convincingly beaten back attempts by British and French forces to take the ground earlier in the year. When the fireball that was to be Vimy Ridge erupted, Roper silently thanked whomever or whatever was responsible for his assignment to machine guns. The machine-gunners were under cover, required only to maintain a killing cover for the infantry whose bodies piled up like dropped dolls as they advanced on the Germans huddled in their concrete bunkers. The Canadians took the hill, leaving almost four thousand dead out of more than ten thousand total casualties. While Roper and his squad were departing for the rear, one young, sadly heroic German soldier rose from the pile of muck and wreckage where he had taken cover and tossed a grenade in a final, quixotic gesture. The grenade exploded while it was still in the air, and shrapnel chewed Roper's left leg from ankle to thigh as he dived for cover. The German boy died in a storm of lead. Roper was operated on and shipped back to England to recuperate. He made a desultory, unsuccessful effort to locate members of his family before returning to Canada.

Within six months of the war ending, Roper recognized what many veterans were learning: the government had had its use of them, now it wished they would disappear. He took a loan out under the Soldier Settlement Act to set up on a mixed farm south of Saskatoon. Two disastrous winters backed his payments up beyond the point where he could make them, and there was nobody offering a second chance. He locked the doors, walked away and confirmed what he had long told himself: put your trust in no one, and you won't be disappointed.

He drifted from the Atlantic to the Pacific, and even to the Arctic. He ventured south into the States and worked in bar rooms and in stockyards in Chicago while the twenties roared all around him. And then, by way of the West Coast, he returned to Vancouver where he found work in the logging camps outside the city, until the Depression hit. Then nobody was working anywhere and the only camps hiring were the twenty-cents-a-day government relief operations that served more as jail-camps to hold potential troublemakers than anything else. Roper did his share of trouble-making. He joined and helped inflame the army of unemployed protesters demanding real work and decent wages who occupied the Vancouver Post Office for six weeks in May and June of 1935. He choked on the tear gas and felt the whips of the Mounties and the Vancouver city cops who finally drove the protesters back onto the streets.

From there, with about a thousand others, he boarded a commandeered freight train for the On To Ottawa Trek, which ended in the Regina Riots on July 1, with a Regina cop being killed and Christ knows how many marchers getting their skulls cracked. By this time Roper had had enough anyway. The squabbling among the leaders of the various democratic and workers-rights groups was looking more and more like just another gaggle of politicians scrambling for power. And the trekkers had been double-crossed by politicians, including Prime Minister Bennett, from the start. Roper asked those around him, so many of them veterans of the war, what they had really expected. What did they really think they were going to get from all the marching and singing of solidarity songs—a fair deal? A square deal? Shit. Believe that, and go looking for leprechauns and pots of gold. The only thing the people in charge were interested in was staying in charge, and keeping you out. The only way the Ropers of the world would ever get a fair deal, or any kind of deal, was when they reached out and grabbed one when it showed up, and never mind who they grabbed it from. Until Roper climbed back into military uniform as a member of the Veterans Guard, nothing had shown up. Now that it had, he was holding on to it with both hands.

- -

The Jeep came up fast toward the store and looked as if it would sail on past but at the last second, with a screech of brake pads, the Jeep wheeled and skidded to a stop in front of Kristin.

"Nearly missed you sitting there," Roper laughed as he climbed out of the Jeep. He pushed back a flop of blonde hair.

Like a kid doing it, Kristin thought, as she studied him. *Some kid.*

"You all right?" Roper said.

She nodded. "Sure. Why wouldn't I be?"

"You looked a bit glum, is all." Roper walked over to the steps. "Nice guy, your father-in-law." He looked around. "Did he go?"

"He went, all right." Roper read events into her tone, and laughed.

"Well, I just thought I'd check on you," Roper said. "What are you...?" He pointed to the writing pad, then quickly raised a hand and added apologetically, "I'm sorry, of course ... " and he turned as if to leave.

"No," Kristin said quickly, "don't rush off, it's all right." She looked down at the steps, then back at Roper.

"I mean, I was just ... I'm so sick of saying the same things over, and not being able to do anything. You know, the same things that seem to make no sense: 'Dearest Gareth, we miss you. ... Dearest Gareth, we hope you are keeping well and that this war will soon be over. ... Dearest Gareth ...'" She shook her head and lowered it, and suddenly she sobbed, "Oh, Christ, what's the use? What the hell is the use?"

Roper hesitated, then reached out and touched her arm. "Hey," he said, softly.

She brushed a tear from her face.

"There's all the use in the world," Roper said. He stepped up and sat down next to her. "Lots of use, Kristin." She turned her face to him. He lifted his hand and dabbed a tear from her cheek. "In the last war we couldn't get enough of it. I wasn't a prisoner, of course, but what I was, it wasn't much better, and all anybody wanted was to hear about the ordinary things at home, just because they *were* ordinary. Just to know that somebody was thinking about them. That they could go into each day knowing there might be a letter at the end of it, telling them what was happening in town, what everybody at home was doing. And it didn't matter how often they heard it. They needed to know things were the same, to know they would be there for them to come back to. It was what kept them going." Roper did not add that he knew this only from observing his comrades, who *did* have families back home.

Kristin nodded, "I know, I know what you're saying. And I try. I try to sound ... happy, you know?" Her hand touched Roper's and he closed his fingers around hers.

"And then I think, oh, Christ, here I am sounding all happy and he's stuck there and God only knows what's happening to him, and the fact is I'm the last thing but happy." She sobbed, and her grip tightened on Roper's hand.

"I just feel so alone. I just feel so lonely." The sobbing deepened and she leaned into him. He placed his arm around her and felt the tremours shifting through her body, and the warmth of her skin through her thin coverall.

"It's all right," he said softly, and his hand moved across her back in small comforting circles. She moved closer to him and placed her head in the sun-warmed hollow of his throat and he continued to stroke her. She lifted her damp face to his and he kissed her. Roper's hands found the soft, receptive curves of her breasts. Her body tightened as his fingers brushed her nipples, and she moved as if to stop him. He let his hand lie still, just barely cupping her breast, and she allowed it to stay. He felt her relax, then he heard her sigh as she pushed toward him again, so he slipped his hand inside her coverall and felt the warm flesh. She gasped. "Not here," she whispered. They rose from the porch and he followed her across the short distance in the evening light to the house behind the store.

"Where's David?" Roper said, his voice husky.

"Ian's," she answered. "He's staying over." She clung to him as they went inside. She led him upstairs to her bedroom.

She wore only a full slip and underwear beneath her coverall and she gasped as Roper found her firm right breast and cupped it in his warm, rough hand. He let his thumb glide over the nipple. She felt the heat rise from her centre and she moaned as he undressed her and lowered her onto the bed.

"Have you got—?" she started, and Roper nodded, yes, and drew a small square package, a military-issue condom, from his pocket and dropped it onto the bed.

She gasped as he slid a hand down across her belly and found the patch of silken hair and gently probed until his finger slid into her soft, fleshy wetness. She moaned as he moved his finger and found the places that promised to bring her to the point of explosion. She moved her hand and felt his cock. She touched it and stroked it, bringing moans of pleasure from Roper. She waited for him to lower himself but instead he kneeled before her and gently eased her legs apart and began kissing her thighs, moving higher with each kiss.

Kristin couldn't believe what she thought he was going to do. She jumped as his hands slid up her body, stroking and finding her breasts. Now one hand was on each of her breasts, the ridged nipples being gently massaged by the flat of each rough palm. Then his face was between her legs and his tongue, hot, was probing. She knew of it but she had never done it. Gareth had never done it.

Roper was licking her now, rhythmically, and she was aflame. Her legs fell apart and she spread them, straining to give him all the entry he wanted. Then she was ready and beginning to cry out and Roper was standing over her, grabbing her hand to guide it to the throbbing, jutting erection. Her hand brushed the ridges and ripples of scars of old wounds. She sought for and found his erection. She closed her hand around it and began to stroke it, quickly, urgently, feeling the ridge of the lower part of the knob as the skin slid back and forth across it, feeling him quiver. He dropped a hand down between her legs and continued, tantalizingly with a finger what he had started with his tongue.

"Now!" she cried out. "Oh, God, now!" And then, frantically, "The thing! Put it on! Put it on!" And she moaned as she fumbled with him and their two hands finally rolled the thin rubber protector before she engulfed him and he plunged deeper and deeper into her. It ended on a high, shrieking cry from Kristin that she muffled by grabbing a handful of bed sheet and pushing it into her mouth. She continued crying out while Roper seemed to grow thicker and harder inside her and finally he released with a shuddering series of driving strokes. He lowered himself onto her where in a moment her rippling orgasm subsided, and he withdrew and lay beside her.

They slept for an hour. Kristin woke first and dreamily touched him. This time it was less urgent, but eventually they found the tide again, riding the giant wave until it crested and they abandoned themselves once more.

When Kristin awoke again, Roper was gone and the sun had set. She rolled over and examined the depression where he had lain beside her, the crumpled, sweat-stained pillow on his side of the bed. She lay back and placed an arm over her eyes.

chapter fifteen

Incident at Willow Creek:
Our findings suggest that Warrant Officer Second Class Bishop was
determined to make life difficult for the prisoner Kruger from the
dangerous moment in the compound, where Kruger chose to contradict him
publicly. It seems clear also that both before and after Kruger did nothing
to justify Bishop's treatment of him, indeed that he did what he could to
avoid confrontation. Bishop's continuing behaviour of escalating abuse
appears to have been what led, inevitably, to the tragic result.

A crew of eight prisoners had unloaded rolls of barbed wire and a
stack of fence posts. Under Joe Kenny's supervision, the first post
holes were being sunk. The hot air was thick with the smell of the
creosote that soaked the butt ends of each eight-foot, four-by-four
red cedar post. Eric Kruger and Dieter Schiller, the young pilot
who had attached himself to the submariner, worked as a pair.
Kruger pulled the heavy work of cranking the post-hole digger
into the baked and rocky earth. The new fencing was to replace
a stretch ripped out by a Harvard trainer from the airbase. The
small plane had run out of gas a few miles short of home and
had put down in a crash-landing that had left the pilot-instructor
horribly embarrassed and his student terrified of ever leaving the
ground again. Schiller, one of the youngest Messerschmidt aces
until his 109 was shot from under him by a hunting RAF Spitfire
and he had bailed out over the coast of northern France, had been
laughing about the Harvard story since they climbed down out of
the trucks. Frequently his laugher was interrupted by prolonged
bouts of coughing, and his face dripped with perspiration. His
job was to scrape out the loose soil and pebbles that rolled back
into the hole as Kruger worked the post-hole digger. They had
set four posts and Kruger was placing a fifth one in place when
Bishop pulled up in a Jeep. He climbed out, all spit and polish
and newly barbered.

Joe Kenny straightened up and affected alertness. He walked
among the prisoners, gesturing, correcting, and keeping an eye on
Bishop, who stood with his feet spread, studying the work.

Kruger avoided looking at Bishop and muttered to Schiller to do the same. They concentrated on planting the cedar post, eye-balling it in line with the previous four. Schiller had shovelled the first lot of earth back into the hole around the base of the post and Kruger was jiggling the post to settle the rubble around it when, from behind them, Bishop spoke.

"Take it out." He was squinting along the short line of posts they had already set.

Schiller stopped what he was doing, and looked at his partner. Kruger's hands rested on the post, which he held upright in the centre of the hole.

"Pardon, Sergeant Major?" said Kruger.

Bishop looked at him, his face forming a patient half-smile, the kind one would reserve for a backward child. "It's not straight, Admiral." The sailor looked puzzled. "The post. It's not in line with the others. Take it out. Fill the hole in, get your line right, dig another hole, and put the post back in, straight. All right?"

The six other prisoners continued with their various tasks, but they listened carefully to Bishop's quietly dangerous tone.

Joe Kenny's eyes flicked from Bishop to the prisoners and back. He edged slowly backwards, one small step at a time, creating distance between himself and Bishop, and confirmed a tight grasp on his rifle. After the last episode in front of the three boys, Roper had told Kenny the army could—and probably would—have held him partly responsible if anyone had been hurt and it had been his rifle involved. He was not about to carry the can for someone like Bishop. He noticed that today Bishop was carrying a sidearm, what looked like a Webley revolver that officers in World War I had carried, in a webbing holster.

Kruger let go of the post and it fell against the side of the hole. Schiller wiped the sweat from his forehead and leaned on his shovel.

"It is almost all stone, rock, right there, Sergeant Major," Kruger said, pointing at the ground. "We had to move it, just centimetres—an inch or two—for the digging."

Bishop said nothing.

"We can make the change, the adjustment, in the next two holes. It will not be noticed, in all this." He hand-swept the prairie that rolled and folded and stretched for miles in every direction, at the sagging fences running into the distance and which seemed to have been erected in whatever shapes and lines the land would accept.

"We can bring it back straight," he reasoned.

Bishop nodded slowly, as though he were considering the German's argument. Then he said, "Like I said, move it."

Joe Kenny shifted his feet, and quietly groaned.

Bishop's eyes switched to Schiller. He cocked his head slightly, inspecting. The young prisoner's breathing was shallow and rapid. His pale-blue shirt was now darkened with sweat.

Kruger lifted the post out of the hole and laid it on the ground. He took the shovel from his partner and carefully scraped the remaining pile of rubble back into the hole and tamped it down. He lifted a heavy pick, which he had been using to start the holes, raised it over his head, and smacked the steel point down into the rocky earth. Sparks flickered, and a rock-chip flew past Bishop's face. Bishop ducked his head. Kruger raised a hand in apology for the accidental near-miss. Bishop only stared.

The German shrugged, spat on his hands and rubbed the spit into his palms. He had the pick raised halfway when Bishop said, "Let him do it."

Kruger halted his pick at shoulder level. "Sergeant Major?"

"I said, let him do it." Bishop nodded to the pilot. "Your little friend."

Kruger shook his head. "It is fine, Sergeant Major. I can do it."

"Give him the fucking pick."

The German lowered the tool. "He is sick, Sergeant Major. He has the ... flu ... influenza. He should not be out here."

Bishop said, "The flu, is it?"

"Yes."

"You the barrack room doctor now, are you?"

"I have seen—" Kruger said.

Bishop cut him off. "More like a nurse, maybe, eh?" He laughed, a short, harsh sound.

"Sergeant Major, he is my friend—"

"Girlfriend, maybe," Bishop said and a cold little smile visited his mouth.

"Sergeant Major—"

"I think he's a fuckin' pansy," Bishop said. "And you don't want him to get his hands dirty. That about it, Admiral? Eh?"

Anger flashed on the German's face, and he fought it down. "You know it is not, Sergeant Major. You know there is nothing like that. You know it." His words were a plea to reason.

"You hear that, private? He's looking out for his little sweetie." Bishop had turned his head and called to Kenny, whose expression betrayed a strong preference to be somewhere else. Kenny was also wishing Roper would get himself here, as he was supposed to.

Bishop turned back to the Germans. "Well, we don't want him to break a finger nail or anything. You get boring them holes, Admiral, and you, Nancy, or whatever the fuck your name is," he said to the puzzled and now worried-looking pilot. "Let me see you moving that shovel."

He made a show of adjusting the webbing belt holding the holstered revolver on his hip, and turned away in dismissal. The other prisoners, who had stopped again to watch, quickly resumed their work.

The pilot asked Kruger what was happening. He glanced at Bishop's back and shook his head, muttering, "*Nichts*. Nothing." He took the pick and started slamming chunks of rock out of the earth. Bishop propped himself against the Jeep and watched.

Kruger dropped the pick, took the shovel, and scooped up a mound of loose earth and rock pieces. He swapped the shovel for the pick, and resumed hacking. Dieter Schiller looked paler by the minute. He swayed, and suddenly sat down on the grass. He ran a hand across his forehead and the sweat dripped through his fingers and fell into the dust at his feet. His face was a pasty clay-white.

Kruger hacked more of the dense earth into rubble. He put the pick down and took up the shovel to shift the loosened material, and a hand took hold of the shovel and held it still.

"I told *him* I wanted to see the shovel move, not you, you asshole," Bishop said.

He pointed a threatening forefinger toward the younger German, who made an effort to lift his head and focus his blurred vision.

"Get up," Bishop said. "On your feet."

"He cannot, Sergeant Major!" Kruger protested.

Schiller struggled to his feet, panting with the effort, and stood, swaying, his head low. Sweat poured down his face and dripped off the end of his nose and chin.

Bishop picked up the shovel and placed it in the young man's hand, and Schiller grabbed it. He used the shovel as a crutch, as his legs threatened to fold under him.

Bishop pointed to the pile of rock and earth that Kruger had loosened. "Dig," he said.

The younger man staggered, then recovered. He aimed the shovel, drove the blade weakly into the pile, and tried to lift the scant amount he had unearthed. The shovel wavered, wobbled, then spilled its contents as Schiller's sweat-slick hands slid down the handle. He crumpled to his knees and crouched, like some wounded creature, with the shovel handle pointed resting on his shoulder. He mumbled something unintelligible, and a shiver rippled over his slight frame.

Bishop tapped his swagger stick against his thigh. He too was sweating heavily, fat drops which beaded on his brow and burst into rivulets that ran down his cheeks. "Get on your feet." He poked the young German with the tip of his swagger stick. "Get up, sissy boy."

"He cannot, Sergeant Major! Look at him!" Eric Kruger protested.

Joe Kenny had cautiously made his way to the spot. He looked down at Schiller, who had turned his face upwards. "Jesus, sir, he's in no shape—"

"Shut up, Private!" Bishop whirled on Kenny. "And get back to your duty."

For a moment it seemed that Kenny might argue. But the burning eyes in the florid face determined his course. He turned and walked back to where he had been.

Bishop returned his attention to the young pilot. He leaned down to him. "Get on your fucking feet," he growled.

Schiller was now on his hands and knees. He nodded his compliance. He lifted one knee from the earth, strained to take his weight on his foot, and again using the shovel as a prop, raised himself part way off the ground.

"Thaaat's right," Bishop crooned. "Uuuup we get."

The German's hand slipped on the shovel shaft. He moaned and grabbed for it, but the shovel fell away from him, and he crashed face down, gasping and sobbing, in the pile of loose earth and rocks.

"You fucker!" Bishop drew back his hobnailed-booted right foot.

"No!" Eric Kruger jumped in between Bishop and the now motionless Dieter Schiller.

- -

Roper saw the three figures as he pulled in off the highway driving a truck loaded with more posts and wire, and a selection of military supplies that Roper knew deserved a better home than sitting unused on a quartermaster's shelves. The truck bounced as the wheels found ruts and rocks, and he fought the spinning steering wheel to keep the vehicle under control. He saw the young German sprawled on the ground and the desperate look on the face of Kruger as the German stepped in front of Bishop, and he saw Bishop's hand drop toward the revolver at his belt.

He rammed his foot down on the gas pedal and sent the truck crashing and bouncing the last forty yards that separated him from the scene. He slammed the truck to a stop inches from Bishop's threatening bulk and jumped down from the cab.

Bishop wheeled, glaring. Roper's mouth tightened as Schiller slowly turned and looked up at him. Roper saw the distress on the man's face.

"What the hell's going on, Jack?" He dropped to one knee beside the young German. He touched Schiller's forehead and his face, feeling the heat rising from the German's body.

He ignored Bishop who was barking, "Don't you 'Jack' me!"

Roper shouted back at him. "The kid's on fire, he's burning up, for Christ's sake! You trying to kill him?"

Roper lifted the violently shivering and sobbing German to his feet. Schiller's shirt was now a black, sodden mess stuck to his skinny frame. Roper half-carried, half-dragged him to the truck.

"You are out of line, Corporal!"

Roper ignored Bishop. "Eric," he said to the sailor, "help me with him, into the truck. He's going back to camp. You too," he said, as Kruger hurried to obey. They lifted the younger man's limp body into the bed of the truck.

"Cover him," Roper ordered, indicating a neat stack of brand-new army blankets sitting in a corner of the truck's bed. "And hold on to him." He climbed into the cab, shoved the gear shift into first, released the emergency brake, and swung the truck into the beginnings of a turn. He leaned from the open window and faced Bishop, whose face was livid.

"One day you'll go too far," Roper said. He swung the wheel and fought it as the truck lurched along the rutted ground. Kruger threw blankets over Schiller and held him down as the truck bounced and swayed.

The rest of the workforce stared after the truck.

Joe Kenny kept his eyes on Bishop and covertly rejoiced in the changing patterns of anger and chagrin that marched across Bishop's beef-red features.

Bishop caught him watching. "What's your problem, Kenny?" He pointed to the remaining prisoners. "Get these assholes back to work, unless you want to pick up a fuckin' shovel yourself?"

Kenny quickly obeyed, knowing very well that Bishop right now would like nothing more than a fresh target to replace the one that Roper had removed.

chapter sixteen

"David! Will you come on, we don't have all day!"

Boy, his mom was grumpy the last couple of days, David thought. Just about anything seemed to set her off.

All he had done this time was stop to look at the model planes and tanks and some new tin soldiers in Mr. Wilson's shop window. He lengthened his stride on the wooden sidewalk along Main Street to catch up to her. She had seemed mad ever since he got back from staying at Ian's place, although he couldn't think of anything that had gone wrong with that. Well, they had tied a can to the cat's tail, and Ian's mother had yelled at Ian for that, but David was pretty sure Mrs. Mackenzie hadn't said anything to his mom about it. And it was Ian's idea, anyway, and his cat.

"In here," his mom said, and steered him through the door of Murray's Shoe Shop. He could have gone in blindfolded and the smell of dozens of pairs of new leather shoes would have told him exactly where he was.

"We'd like to see some boots, please, Patsy," his mom said to the clerk, who was the Murrays' daughter.

"Hello, David," Patsy said. "Almost time for school again, I guess? Couple of weeks or so? Okay, let's see how your toes look today, shall we?"

She always talked to him as if he were about five, David thought, but he smiled anyway and stepped up happily enough to the machine, which was tucked up against the back wall of the shop below several shelves of shiny black and brown boots and shoes.

"Up here," Patsy said, and David stepped up on to the machine's flat base, then shuffled his feet until they were directly under the box with the glass frame on the top. He held on to the two handles at the side while Patsy made sure his feet were exactly placed under the glass.

"Ready?" Patsy said, and David nodded, a little tickle of excitement shooting through him as the light went on under the glass plate.

"There, what do you think?" Patsy asked, and David chuckled as he looked down at the X-ray picture of the bones of his feet in a greenish light bordered by a dark fuzzy area that must be his well-worn shoes.

"I think you're about ready for the next size," Patsy said, nodding and studying the skeleton bones. David had seen a real skeleton in the museum in Lethbridge once, and the bones had looked exactly like this. Ian said if somebody had X-ray eyes, they would be able to see right through girls' dresses, past their underpants and everything.

"See," Patsy said, "the bones are a bit pushed together there, your big toe and the one next to it. What do you think, Mrs. Evans?" she asked. His mom leaned over, laughing as David wiggled his toes and the bones moved, and he looked up at her and laughed, glad she wasn't still grumpy.

"I think you're right, Patsy," Kristin said. "He's growing, all right," and she rumpled his hair as David continued examining his toes, moving his feet out to the side until half the bones seemed to disappear, then sliding them back into view again.

David tried on two pairs of boots and his mom said she thought the second pair looked the best.

"How do they feel?" she asked.

David frowned a moment. "Well, all right, I guess, but I think we should check them on the machine."

His mom laughed at Patsy Murray and said, "Imagine that."

David remounted the machine and after a lengthy examination and much toe wiggling, said, "Well, they're big enough, but they feel stiff."

"You'll get used to them," his mom said, in the same kind of voice she used when she said things like, "Well, that's life." David sat on a chair with his feet up on a sloped stool and undid the laces, smelling the new leather, while his mom paid Patsy at the counter.

"And we polish these, every day," she said, poking him with a reminding finger and making him giggle as he pulled the door open, making the bell ring over their heads as they left the store.

An army truck had parked next to the board sidewalk while they were in the shoe store. A heavy footstep sounded behind them and a uniformed figure moved alongside.

"Morning," Steve Roper said, and David noticed how his mom

jumped at the sound. "Hiya, Davie." Roper grinned down at him. "How ya doin'?"

David returned the smile, his glance jumping from Roper back to the truck, a few paces away.

David's mom suddenly got busy checking the inside of her shopping bag, and glancing up and down the sidewalks on each side of the street.

"I was in Calgary for a couple of days," Roper said, and David's mom replied, "That's a good place to be." David was paying more attention to the truck and its cargo. He was only vaguely aware that Roper was talking to his mom, that their voices were low, and that his mom was shaking her head and saying, "No, absolutely not!"

The German sailor had put his head around the truck's cab and was watching the three of them. He smiled when he caught David looking and suddenly went cross-eyed. David laughed to see it.

"...was a mistake," his mom was saying to Roper in the background, her voice low. "No, I don't care what you say, " and Roper was answering, "You know you do," in a teasing way.

David chuckled as the German rolled his eyes and put a goofy smile on his face.

Suddenly David's hand was being grabbed and his mom was shoving him along the sidewalk, ducking away from Roper, who had reached out a hand to her. Laughing, Roper called out to her, "Hey, don't go away mad!"

She yanked him on past the truck, where the German said, "Hello," as they swept by. As she turned sharply into Arnason's Clothing Store, she snapped, "Who was that?"

"Just Jerries," David said. He added, "They're all right, some of them." His mother seemed not to hear. She was looking out the store window at the truck where Roper was climbing into the cab.

"What did Corporal Roper say?" David asked.

"What? Oh, I don't know, some rubbish about being away or something. As if it matters to anybody."

David had been wondering, and he was going to ask her, if she thought his dad got to go into town in trucks where he was, like the Jerries did here. But he decided, with her in the mood she was in again, he better leave it.

chapter seventeen

Incident at Willow Creek:
Following the work site incident involving Warrant Officer Second Class Jack Bishop and the two prisoners, Kruger and Schiller, it seems clear that Bishop began a campaign of harassment of Kruger that far exceeded any treatment of prisoners considered acceptable. It is our opinion that Cpl. Steve Roper should have taken action (by submitting a report on what was happening) to put an end to the situation, and that it was to serve his own particular interests that he failed to do so. In pursuing this reasoning, it could be concluded that Roper in fact could have prevented the final tragedy had he had the will, and the conscience, to do so.

Liz Thomas looked up as a gust of wind splattered rain against the window panes behind her. At least it had held off for the burial. She returned to the report. This Corporal, Roper, sounded like someone the world could have done without. He could have stopped whatever tragedy they were talking about, but chose not to, by the sound of it to save his own skin. *Tragic for who?*

- -

The two chess players lifted their heads as the barrack room door opened. Their eyes locked across the upturned apple box on which their chessboard rested as Bishop stepped through the door. Bishop glanced down at the two faces, pleased by the sudden guardedness, the apprehension he saw there.

"Carry on," he said, and the pair relaxed. They exchanged looks and their heads turned and followed Bishop's progress as his measured pace took him the length of the sixteen-bed hut, eight bed-spaces along each wall, past the neatly made-up cots with the simple locker and small table beside each bed.

Eric Kruger had looked up as Bishop entered the room and his jaw had tightened. But he resumed writing the letter he had started, keeping the handwriting as small as possible while still keeping it legible, in order to squeeze as many words as he could onto the single sheet of paper. Beside him on a wooden night stand was a small framed black-and-white photograph of a young woman and a little boy. The woman was full-bosomed, with a slim waist. Her blonde hair was done in a bun, with wisps escaping. She wore a flowered frock with a narrow white belt at the waist. She shaded her eyes as she laughed at the camera. The boy, dark-haired and chubby-faced, was dressed in shorts, short sleeved shirt, and a diamond patterned sleeveless pullover. He came to just above the woman's knee and had one small arm wrapped around her leg. The thumb of his other hand was fixed firmly in his mouth. Kruger felt a knife in his heart each time he looked at the snap and recalled how they had laughed and made faces as he tried to get the two of them to keep still for the picture. He wrote a letter each week, describing his activities, sending his unending love to Michelle, his wife, and Hans, his son, who would now be eight. The thought of them sustained him. He had met and married Michelle Primeau in her native Paris, and they had loved and laughed in a two-room flat on the outskirts of Berlin, where Hans was born during one of Kruger's extended leaves from his passenger ship. They had decided he would look for a shore job, one that would bring him home each night to his family, like normal people. And then the little demagogue had decided to redraw the map of Europe.

In the eighteen months since his Unterseeboote was depth-charged by a Royal Canadian Navy Corvette in the frigid waters of the Cabot Strait, and he and five other survivors from the U-boat crew were taken prisoner, Kruger had not received a single reply to his letters. The Red Cross had been unable to supply any word about his wife and son. He lived in the belief that Michelle had been able to get herself and Kris to a place of safety, and that he would find them when the war was over. His thoughts about them, his plans for their future together, were his escape, his refuge from the other thoughts, the ones that said, yes, but here is the reality.

It was two days since Schiller had collapsed at the work site. Kruger had returned the same day with Roper, and had been back at the fencing job since. Bishop had not been back to the site, but he had made his presence doubly felt here, around the camp. Once, on the evening of that first day, Kruger saw Bishop talking to Roper on the steps of the orderly room. And it was decidedly Bishop doing the talking, twice prodding Roper in the chest with a finger, driving home his words. The anger, the resentment at Bishop's tone and actions, was evident in Roper's face, but his mouth had stayed shut. Roper was uncharacteristically quiet as he drove the prisoners to and from the work site on the following day, his usual easy smile and jokes noticeably missing. But his mood had lightened by this morning, when they had gone out again, and Eric's day had been further brightened by his brief exchange with the boy from the roadside gas pump and shop, when Roper had stopped the truck in town. Roper seemed to have got very short shrift from the mother, and when Eric said, "So, Corporal, the lovely lady seems annoyed with you," Roper had grinned and said, "Fuck you, sailor," and they had laughed.

There was no thought of laughter now, as Bishop slowed his heavy steps and stopped before the German's cot. Bishop carried his ever-present swagger stick, this time clasped behind his back, horizontal between his hands.

Kruger finished writing a sentence and looked up. Bishop's face was without expression. The German returned to his letter, his pencil poised.

Bishop flicked his swagger stick out and rapped it on the taut blanket covering the cot, close to the German. "So, where's the Red Baron?" he asked.

Kruger looked up again, then over at the next cot and at Bishop's stick. "He is in the sick bay, Sergeant Major," he said. And then, with every sense he possessed urging him to leave the matter right there, he added, "That must not be a surprise to you, I think."

Bishop's forehead wrinkled as he considered his response. By now, the German should be well-tamed, not coming back with smart-ass answers. But if he still needed convincing, he was in the right place and with just the right man.

Kruger held Bishop's stare for a moment, then he glanced away, to the picture of his wife and son.

Bishop followed the direction of Kruger's glance. He lifted the point of his swagger stick and held it a fraction of an inch away from the framed picture. "What do we have here?"

"That is my family, Sergeant Major. My wife and my son."

"Ah." Bishop seemed satisfied.

Kruger looked deliberately away from the picture, as if doing so would pull Bishop's attention away, too.

Bishop leaned forward and touched the picture frame with the tip of the stick. "Another little Nazi Brown Shirt. That right?"

Kruger carefully placed the sheet of writing paper face down on his bed and set the stub of pencil on top of it. "That is my son," he said. "He is now eight years old. That is my wife with him. I do not know where they are."

He spoke the last words quietly, almost to himself, an affirmation of the unremitting sense of loss that ruled his waking thoughts.

Bishop moved the swagger stick point onto the young woman's image. "Do you ever wonder what she's up to?" he said mildly.

"Up to? I do not know what—"

"While you're away, for Christ's sake! What she's up to, what she's doing. What do you think she's doing while you're stuck over here?"

Boots scraped on the floor at the far end of the hut, and Bishop and the German both turned to see the two chess players leaving. Bishop returned his attention to Kruger. "Well?"

The German shook his head. "I wish I knew that, Sergeant Major."

"I'll bet you do," Bishop said. He smiled. "I'll bet *I* know."

Eric Kruger said nothing.

"You see, Admiral," Bishop went on, his tone now that of a man sharing a confidence. "The way it is, there's a whole lot of young SS stallions over there, and I wonder if you ever think that she might be servicing a few?"

He waited for a response, and when none came, he added, "I mean that she's probably getting fucked stupid by your Nazi comrades, because you can't do anything for her from here, can you?" His smile remained.

Kruger had no difficulty understanding Bishop's message. He looked Bishop up and down, from his shiny boots to squared-off cap, as if close study might provide some explanation of the character under the clothing.

"I'll bet she's on her back for them every night," Bishop continued. "Know what we call them around here, tarts like her?" And he neither expected nor waited for a response. "The camp bicycle! Know why? 'Cos every body rides it!" And he laughed aloud. "You know what else, Admiral?"

Kruger shrugged and a half smile tugged at the corner of his mouth. For a second the smile seemed to puzzle Bishop. He frowned, then continued.

"What else is, that he," and he rapped the image of the boy in the picture, "is likely standing at the door taking their money as they line up. How do you like that?"

The German shrugged again, and the smile was back.

Bishop glared. "Do you understand what I've been saying?" he shouted. "Do you get the picture?"

Kruger nodded. "I understand, Sergeant Major. But the fact that you say it, does not make it so, does it?" And the smile along with the words suggested the unspoken rest of the thought: *the fact that you say anything does not make it so, and more likely the opposite would be the case.*

Then Kruger laughed. It had started with the little smile and now it became a quiet, low series of chuckles as he looked up at Bishop, with his beefy face shiny with sweat, his peaked hat rigidly, correctly in place, the crisply ironed khaki shirt, now sweat-stained with patches of black spreading from the armpits out. He laughed at everything bizarre and ugly and stupid that Bishop represented, and his laughter grew louder and higher. But then the laughter stopped and he waited to see what Bishop would do next. There was, certainly, more to come.

Bishop had been astonished by the laughter. As it continued, he was perplexed. And then it came to him, incredulously, that *the German was actually laughing at Jack Bishop. Not at what Jack Bishop had said. At what Jack Bishop was. A fucking German, laughing at Jack Bishop!*

He waited until the laughter dried up. He tapped his swagger stick against his thigh, and said, quietly, "That was comical, was it, Admiral?"

The German shook his head. He wanted no more conversation. He said nothing.

"I mean," Bishop continued, "I tell you that that woman of yours there is a prostitute, spreading her legs for the German army. I say that your little Nazi there is likely her pimp. And you fucking laugh? Is that right?"

The German closed his eyes and shook his head again.

Bishop smiled down at him.

"Well, you know what I think?" He raised his eyebrows, with the air of a man who had just solved a difficult problem. "I think that *you* were takin' the piss out of me." He nodded, satisfied with the avenue that had now opened up for him. "Is that what you were doin', Admiral? Takin' the piss out of the Sergeant Major? Is that it?"

Bishop tapped his swagger stick on the iron end of the cot. "Well?"

Kruger looked at Bishop, and away.

"Right then," Bishop said. "I'll take that as a yes. And I'll show you what it gets you. Get on your feet."

Kruger stood and picked up the half-finished letter and the pencil stub.

"You won't need them," Bishop said.

The German slid open the drawer in the nightstand and placed the letter and pencil inside. He picked up the framed photograph and placed it on the high shelf in his locker and closed the locker.

"That's it," Bishop said. "Nice and neat and tidy. That's how we like things." He pointed down the length of the barrack hut with his swagger stick. "Outside, and I'll show you neat and fuckin' tidy."

Bishop marched the German the length of the hut, through the door at the end of the building, down the three steps to the meticulously raked crushed rock path, and along the path to an open area behind the camp cookhouse and mess hall. A stack of firewood split by prisoners, a good four-to-five cords, sat next to the cookhouse wall. Bishop pointed to the stack.

"I think that would look better over there," he said, and indicated a clear area about twenty yards away. "I want it moved, Admiral. Every bit of it, and stack it, neat and tidy. Understand?"

Kruger looked at the hill of wood. "Yes, Sergeant Major."

"Get on with it," Bishop said.

The German walked over and picked up an armful of split logs, stepped across to the cleared spot and set them down, neatly, and returned and filled his arms again.

"That's the idea," Bishop said. "That's perfect." He checked a heavy watch on his left wrist. "I'll be back to check on you later."

Kruger watched Bishop leave. He examined the stack of split firewood and shrugged. He added his armful to the new location and returned to the stack and picked up another load.

Bishop returned two hours later. Kruger's face and neck streamed with sweat. He had moved all but a couple of armfuls of the split logs and had placed them in perfectly squared stacks.

Bishop nodded his approval, while Kruger watched him warily. "That is excellent, Admiral," Bishop said. "Excellent." He pointed to the last few logs left in the original location. "Just finish them off," he said, "then tell the cook I said he could get you some supper."

The relief was clear on the German's face. "Thank you, Sergeant Major."

Bishop smiled. He said, "Then, when you've had your supper, put it all back where it was." He turned and marched away.

chapter eighteen

Incident at Willow Creek:

In making the outlandish suggestion in his report at the time,that Cpl. Roper somehow should be held accountable for the unfortunate happening concerning the prisoner Peter Weiss at the farm of Henry and Martha Jensen, Warrant Officer Bishop seems to have been doing nothing more than trying to prepare a retaliatory case against Roper in the event that Roper did indeed decide to take action against Bishop's continuing abusive treatment of the prisoner Kruger. While Roper evidently had a specific arrangement with Jensen within the general practice of assigning prisoners to work -- and allegedly other, illegal, arrangements outside of regular channels -- he cannot reasonably be said to have contributed to the outcome. Roper was acting within his mandate in assigning the POWs who in his judgment were appropriate for a particular situation. Weiss would have been deemed suitable under all standard criteria for short-term, live-in work at the Jensen farm.

Liz Thomas tried to picture these men. Bishop sounded the worst by far, but Roper obviously was no bargain either, if the Provost Corps Major's report was accurate. Wheeling and dealing with farmers and prisoners of war, and involved with an "unfortunate incident" involving now this other prisoner, named Weiss. Was this incident related to "the tragedy"? Maybe it *was* "the tragedy". But where did her mother, Kristin Evans, come into it? She read on.

chapter nineteen

Peter Weiss examined the fresh stack of pancakes on his plate, runny with butter and maple syrup, the heap of crisped bacon and browned sausage on the serving dish, and laughed as Martha Jensen urged him to eat more.

"Come on, Peter, you've hardly touched anything," she chided.

"Eight pancakes, already!" the young POW protested. "And many sausage, and—"

"Well, you're still a growing boy," Martha chuckled. "Go on, get a bit more into you!"

From the other side of the table Henry Jensen beamed at the bantering between his wife and the young German. Two weeks now and it seemed as if they had never been without the boy. Henry's smile softened as he watched Martha ruffle the boy's hair. Maybe, Henry thought, this was one odd way of bringing some balance to a world where balance seemed in short supply. More than anything, Martha had wanted children of her own, but there had been none. There had been the illness, the terrible, gripping fear, then the hysterectomy, which had returned her to him, for which he had thanked his good Lord. But they would never have children. Still, Henry had Martha. And now they had Peter.

Peter Weiss had heard the stories from other prisoners sent to work on local farms, some good, some anything but good—water and bread and cheese for every meal, and virtually no rest during twelve- and fourteen-hour days. He had even tried to talk Corporal Roper out of sending him at all, asking instead to be kept on the construction crews in and around Camp 10, where he at least knew what to expect, and how to avoid the worst of it. But Roper had said he had promised these particular clients one of his best workers, and that was that.

At the first meal in the Jensen house Peter had looked around to see who else might be coming in to deal with the mountain of food Martha Jensen had prepared. There was beef, chicken, potatoes, vegetables, salads, hot bread, and what seemed like dozens of cakes and cookies. Nobody else had shown up, and Peter had done his best to make his way through the piles of food. He had been doing so at every mealtime since.

He had marvelled when Martha showed him the room she had prepared for him: a double bed with a fat, soft mattress and brightly patterned quilt, a chest of drawers and a wardrobe, and a view out of a broad window across the rippling acres of hay and maturing wheat that covered the half section that was the Jensen farm.

At the end of the first week of Martha's meals, she had joked with Peter about how he was filling out.

"They won't know you when you get home, Peter."

His face clouded, and he lowered his knife and fork. "*Nein* ... no, there is now no home."

Martha stared across the table at Henry. They had already touched on this briefly, in their bed at night, with Peter asleep in his room across the landing. Her husband shook his head—let it go, he'd said, unless the boy wants to talk about it.

Peter continued, working to fit the English words into his German sentence forms. "*Ich habe* ... I have ... no more ... a home," he said. "*Alles* ... all is ... *tot* ... is all dead ... in the bombs." He looked at each of them in turn.

"Dear God," Martha murmured. And then, in a rare burst of profanity, "God damn them all anyway!" Then, "You have a home, Peter. You have a home here. Right?" she said, across the table to Henry.

"That's for sure," Henry confirmed. "Though I'm not sure how we can—"

"We'll find a way," Martha said. "You understand, Peter? You understand what we're saying? You might have to go back to the camp, but not if I can prevent it. There's more than enough work to keep you out here, and Steve Roper might just find it in his best interests to make sure that happens. Once this is all over, you won't have to go back to Germany if you don't want to, not if I have to hide you in the damned hay loft. All right, Peter? You understand all that?"

Peter Weiss nodded and blinked away a tear. "*Ja* ... yes, I understand."

"And what do you think?"" Henry asked.

"I think it is ... *wunderbar*! I think I would want to stay, yes!"

"That settles that, then," Martha said, and she piled more bacon onto the boy's plate, while Henry grinned and winked at him from across the table. Peter looked around the spacious kitchen as if seeing everything for the first time.

They finished the meal and Peter wiped the last of it from his lips. He and Henry set off for the hayfield where they had been mowing since six that morning.

Black smoke belched from the exhaust as Peter started the aged tractor. Two more circuits of the field and it would be done. The weather forecast said they could leave it lying to dry for two or three more days.

Henry waved Peter to start and the young man lowered the mower blade and started rolling down the outside of the remaining stand of hay. Henry was heading into Willow Creek for some odds and ends and, on orders from Martha, a couple of new shirts for Peter.

"He's not going to wear that damned prisoner patch in my house!" she'd said.

Henry was in the truck and about to press the starter when he heard the tractor motor being revved, then dying, revved hard again, and dying.

The rear engine-seal, he knew for sure. He had been hoping the bloody thing would hold up a little longer, knowing there was every chance that it wouldn't. The revving was Peter trying to find the power that was lost because the oil was leaking into the clutch, which was slipping. The harder Peter worked the engine, the more oil found its way into the clutch, and the more the clutch slipped. Shit.

Henry climbed down from the truck and saw that Peter had probably worked out what the problem was, because the lad was already doing the right thing; he had lifted the mower blade and was babying the tractor up along the edge of the stubble.

That was another good thing about the kid, he rarely needed to be told what to do. He had enough common sense for any two people his age. Henry wasn't as confident as Martha that they would be able to keep Peter. At least not right away. But by God … if they could …

The tractor shuddered to a stop, the engine quitting with one last sigh, as it came alongside the flatbed.

"*Ist kaput*, Henry," Peter said, looking down from his perch on the burlap-cushioned iron seat. "Dead," he added, waving a hand helplessly out toward the hay field and the remaining crop. "*Gott damn!*" he said and Henry laughed and agreed.

Henry scratched his head. "Thing's been running on hope and horse shit luck all summer. We're going to have to yank that engine," he said. "Take out the motor." He mimed the proposed action and the German nodded quickly.

"Sure, we fix it."

Between them they removed the mower attachment and dropped it in the stubble. They rigged a towing chain and, with Peter in the tractor seat and Henry driving the truck, they headed back to the farm.

"Get the jack," Henry told Peter. "I'll get the pulley rigged."

An hour later, they'd placed a jack under the transmission, loosened the bolts around the transmission and engine, and wheeled the separated front end of the tractor forward to allow access. They secured the engine with three wraps of chain, and hoisted it on the pulley. Two hours later, Henry crawled out from under the engine, his face red from the effort of working in the confined space, and mottled with oil spots.

"There, good as new, for a bit anyway," Henry said, wiping his hands with a rag, then patting the engine where it swung in its chain cradle.

"Like new," Peter agreed proudly, ignoring the three raw knuckles he had collected loosening bolts.

"Might as well stick new plugs in while we're at it," Henry said, turning toward the spread of tools lying on the deck of the flatbed.

Peter ducked under the block with a rag in his hand. He was about to wipe away some remaining oil streaks when a sound, an odd kind of creaking noise came from the centre chain bearing the engine block's weight.

"Peter!" Henry yelled. Just as the young man lifted his head in response to the shout, the weakened chain link gave way. There was a rattling, ratcheting sound as the released chain whipped and lashed around the engine, and a sickening, crunching thud as the dead weight of the engine dropped across Peter's chest and pinned him to the dry, summer-hard ground.

Frothing blood sprayed from his mouth and nose. Henry, as though running through deep mud, lurched toward him, screaming, "Peter! Jesus! Peter!"

He reached the boy and grabbed the engine block, vainly trying to move it. Henry fell to his knees. His hands fluttered uselessly as he touched the boy and moaned, "Peter, oh, Peter!"

The young German's eyes flickered and, in a whisper, he uttered his last word, "Henry."

chapter twenty

Incident at Willow Creek:

From discussions with a number of Willow Creek citizens, the funeral service for the prisoner Weiss and his interment in the local cemetery was generally approved of, likely as a sign of respect for the Jensens and their place in the community. Initial objections to the plan came from Sergeant Major Bishop, who cited the reports of the murder in early June of more than 130 members of units of the 3rd Canadian Infantry Division by soldiers of the 12th S.S. Panzer (Hitler Youth) division. Bishop withdrew his objections when Wing Commander P.T. Langdon showed an interest in the airbase being represented at the ceremony. The wing commander pointed to the incident last year in Lingren, West Germany, where the German military provided a funeral with full military honours for a group of Allied airmen who had died when their plane crashed.

So the prisoner, Weiss, had died. This surely must be the tragedy they were referring to, and the charges against Roper must have to do with this. Right. Although earlier the provost major had said that Roper was quite correct in what he had done by placing the prisoner at, what was it? Jensen's? Yes, their farm. So what had he done wrong to be facing charges?

Liz flicked to the last page of the report, to the sloping handwriting.

"Kristin: I got hold of this report from one of my friends and I thought you should have it. Not to open old wounds, but just to let you know how it turned out, which I'm sure you would want to know. I've addressed it to the bank, as with the other stuff. The shop is holding its own, thanks. Love always, M."

Liz sighed, shook her head, and rubbed her eyes. She put the papers down. Was "M" a man or a woman? What old wounds? What shop?

- -

David had never seen the Willow Creek United Church completely full. But then, he had never been to a funeral before. He was supposed to have gone to John Thompson's funeral but had started throwing up in the morning and his mom had made him stay home. John had been hit by an army truck when he ran out into the street in Lethbridge. They had laid him out the next day, in a coffin on his bed, and all the neighbours had been invited in by the Thompsons to see him and to say goodbye. John was about a year older than David, but he looked younger in the coffin, David remembered. And a bit smaller. But otherwise not much different, for being dead. Just very still. David's mom hadn't wanted him to see the body, but she had finally given in. Mrs. Thompson gave everybody a cookie as they left.

David glanced over his shoulder. From where he was sitting, on the aisle, he could look back and see Ian four rows behind, sitting with his mom. When Ian and his mom first came into the church and sat down, Ian leaned forward to catch David's attention and started doing his act of old man Dorney hanging from the ceiling. His mother caught him and smacked him a loud crack across the head. David's mom ducked her head down and put her hands up to her face because she was laughing, and everybody else was looking very serious.

The coffin was at the front of the church, with bunches of flowers on the closed lid. David couldn't remember the dead man especially, just knew he was one of the Germans and had been killed in an accident out at the Jensens' place. Mr. and Mrs. Jensen were sitting in the front pew and Mrs. Jensen kept dabbing her eyes with a white handkerchief with little blue flowers on it.

One side of the church was filled with Germans. David counted thirty of them. A member of the Veterans Guard sat at the end of each of the German pews. One of them was Corporal Roper, who had nodded at them when they came in. The day before David had heard his mother say to Corporal Roper, at the gas pump, "Of course it's not your fault, how can it be your fault?" and Roper had said, "Well, some would blame me, for putting him there." And his mother had said, "It's just bad luck, is all it is. If it hadn't been him it would have been somebody else. There's always a wrong place or a wrong time."

"Or a right one," he had said, and laughed.

Roper had smiled at her today, but David noticed she didn't smile back.

Next to Roper was the German that Bishop had pointed the rifle at that day, the sailor, who made faces whenever David saw him. He had smiled at David when he caught his eye across the aisle, and winked. There seemed to be quite a lot of smiling, for a funeral, David thought. Although the German's smile had seemed a bit sad. He looked down to the very back of the Germans' side of the church, and turned his head quickly back when he caught Sergeant Major Asshole glaring at him from a seat by the door.

David turned to the front just as Rev. Warren took his place at the pulpit. He had his long black gown on with the cross of white ribbon at the throat, and he coughed so that everybody would know he was ready. He started reading from the Bible, about eternal God. "Jesus said I am the resurrection and the life," he said, which was about when Jesus had come back from being dead. David hoped they had checked to make sure the man in the coffin was really dead. He had read a report in the *Calgary Herald* about an old man who had died and been put in a coffin, but he hadn't really died. When they were getting ready to bury him somebody heard noises coming from the coffin and they opened it and the old man was still alive, although he died for good a week later. That night, David dreamed about being locked in a coffin.

The pastor said they would now sing hymn number 662. David picked the hymnal out of the rack on the back of the pew in front of him and found the hymn as the organist started up, and then everybody joined in, with Mr. Warren's deep voice leading the singing,

Oh, God, our help in ages past, Our hope in years to come ...

Most of the singing came from the Willow Creek people, but one or two of the Germans kept up with it, including the sailor, David noticed. At the end of the hymn the sailor closed his eyes and stood very still for a while.

"Let us pray," Rev. Warren said. There was a lot of shuffling as people bent forward and lowered their heads.

"Eternal God on high who lovest us with an everlasting love and canst turn the shadow of death into the light of a new day ... "

David was pretty sure Rev. Warren said, "canst." He wondered if the prayer meant that God loved the Germans as well, or if the reverend was just being nice because all the Jerries were in his church.

It was sure taking a long time. Rev. Warren announced he would read the scripture lesson, and then went on to Psalm 121, and Psalm 123, and then Romans Eight, which made David think of the pictures in the social studies book at school. Roman centurians with swords and shields and armour that looked more like skirts, and the helmets with plumes on them and the bit that came down and covered the nose, and the sandals below the leg-armour that came up to the knees. Probably, Rev. Warren used that because the German was a soldier.

Then the reverend gave a sermon, something he always seemed to like doing, but this time he wasn't talking about what you should or shouldn't do, or going to heaven. He talked about Henry and Martha Jensen and how they had opened their hearts and their home to a young man from a foreign land who was supposed to be their enemy but who they had treated more like a son.

Rev. Warren stopped after every couple of sentences and smiled and waited, and David thought he was waiting for the talking among the Germans, of which there seemed to be quite a lot going on for a funeral, to stop. But gradually David realized that the talking was a couple of the Germans telling the others what Rev. Warren was saying, and that's why he kept stopping and starting.

He finished his sermon and said they would now say the Lord's Prayer, which they did, and everybody said, "Amen" at the end.

Out in the cemetery, the Germans gathered at one side of the grave, in proper ranks, and the Willow Creek people on the other side. Rev. Warren said, "God is our refuge and our strength. Into God's keeping we commend our brother here departed ... earth to earth, ashes to ashes, dust to dust. " Then four of the Germans lowered the coffin on ropes into the grave.

David stared at the coffin as it disappeared from sight. When the coffin was in the grave, David was surprised to see Corporal Roper's pal, Private Kenny, step smartly out to the front, carrying a bugle. Then, while all the Germans and the Veterans Guard men stood to attention, Private Kenny played the "Last Post" and only wobbled a bit on the next to last note, which made him grin a bit when he finished.

Not all of the Veterans Guard stood to attention, David noted. Bishop didn't. He stood with his thumbs hooked into his belt on each side, with his swagger stick held in his left hand. As soon as Joe Kenny finished playing, Bishop said loudly to Corporal Roper, "Right, corporal, let's get this shower back into the trucks and on the road. We've wasted enough time here."

His words carried across the grave. David knew that if looks could really kill, the one that Mrs. Jensen sent back to Bishop would have done the trick.

"Just a minute, Sarn't Major," Corporal Roper said, and he nodded across the open grave. Ian's mom had stepped out from the ranks of townspeople. She dropped a small bunch of flowers into the grave and David heard a soft plop as the flowers landed on the coffin. Ian's mom then walked over to Mrs. Jensen and put an arm around her and hugged her. The she turned to Mr. Jensen and patted him on the arm and gave him a quick little kiss on the cheek. David saw Mr. Jensen wipe his eyes.

Then to David's surprise his mom stepped forward and did the same thing with a small bunch of flowers he hadn't known she was carrying. Then women from all through the crowd were step-ping forward and dropping posies into the grave, and each went in turn to the Jensens and each said something or just touched them on the arm before carrying on.

"*Danke*—thank you," a voice said from the German side of the grave. David saw it was the sailor who had spoken and that his words were directed at David's mom. She nodded, then looked away. And then there was "*Danke*" and "Thank you" coming from all the Germans. David saw at least two of the Germans wiping tears off their faces.

Bishop broke the moment, pushing past Roper and facing the Germans and pointing to the three trucks parked on the road outside the graveyard.

"At the double!" Bishop snapped. David saw Corporal Roper shrug and kind of smile at the German sailor, who nodded then turned with the others to leave.

As the trucks drove off, several of the Germans raised their hands and kept them raised until the trucks were out of sight. Bishop brought up the rear of the convoy, driving a Jeep.

"I didn't know you were going to do that," David said, as he and his mom walked toward home.

She gave a little laugh. "I wasn't really sure myself 'til the last minute. It was Moira Mackenzie's idea, for Henry and Martha. I think it was kind of nice."

David nodded. He could hardly wait to get home and take his tie off. He hated wearing ties, but his mom always made him put one on for church. He kicked a rock off the street and under the sidewalk, and noticed the mark it had left on the fresh polish on his new boots. His mom didn't seem to notice.

"I think the Jerries liked it," he said.

They walked on past the stores, all of them closed and many with blinds down against the sun.

"I think they did," his mom agreed.

chapter twenty-one

Incident at Willow Creek:
There appears to have been an incident involving the boy, David Evans,
the prisoner Kruger, and Warrant Officer Second class Jack Bishop, shortly
after the funeral for the prisoner Weiss. Details are very sketchy, as other
prisoners either did not witness the incident, or were not prepared to say
that they did. Mrs. Evans reported one version of it as told to her by the boy.

Liz Thomas re-read the short paragraph. Mrs. Evans? Which Mrs.
Evans? Her mother, Kristin? Of course not. One of her mother's
cousins? Why didn't the Provost Corps major have "the boy's"
report himself? Surely the boy could have been spoken to personally? Was the boy, David Evans, the same boy who was in the
family group picture? And the mother had to be one of the other
Evans women, if that's who one of them was. She looked at the
picture again. The boy had Evans family features, all right, but
maybe he wasn't unlike Liz's mother, either, in some respects.
The nose ... but oh, hell, you could make kids' pictures seem to
look like anybody you wanted to, with a little imagination. She
put the report down and picked through the other papers from
the deposit box. She looked at the wedding invitation, with its
embossed bells and ribbons. The invitation was to the marriage
of Moira Mackenzie and Steve Roper, to take place on April 10,
1948. There was a note.

> Kristin: I know you can't be here, but wish
> me well. I think Steve will make a good
> husband—and they're in short supply around
> here since the base closed! P.S. I wrote this
> before the big day. Now it's a week later, so I
> can send you this photo. We went to Banff for
> the honeymoon!

The snapshot showed a woman wearing a two-piece suit and a
huge smile and carrying a bouquet of mixed blooms. The man
beside her—the infamous Steve Roper, it must be—was in a double-
breasted suit with a rose in his button-hole. He was wearing one of

those hats the British called a trilby and the Americans a fedora. She wondered what Canadians called them. She had a fanciful thought that she knew almost enough about Roper to make his face seem familiar.

Liz opened a small envelope and took out two sheets of writing paper. The date at the head of the letter was twenty-six years after the wedding, and the address was Kensington Road, Calgary:

> Dear Kristin. It's been a long time since I wrote, and this is a sad one. Steve died a week ago.

Liz shivered involuntarily, and felt goosebumps on her flesh. She swallowed the rest of her sherry, and read on:

> Of course as you know he was a good bit older than me, thirteen years in fact. It was a heart attack, and quick, thankfully.

chapter twenty-two

Bishop mopped up the last drops of undercooked egg yolk with a wedge of thickly buttered toast. He caught the expression on his wife's face and wiped the excess drippings with the back of his hand. He licked the residue off his fingers.

Helen Bishop turned her head away.

"What's the matter now?" Bishop spat out the words.

She studied him for a second. "Matter?" she said. And then, brightly, "Why should anything be the matter? You came home legless drunk as usual last night, put me on the floor, but you couldn't do anything, so you took it out on me, like you always do." She touched a finger to an angry bruise not quite hidden under her face powder. "Then you threw up on the counter and in the sink, and then you passed out on the sofa."

He glowered at her. She was exaggerating as she always did. And she wasn't finished.

"Then you got up, pissed all over the bathroom floor."

Bishop hated women swearing, particularly bathroom language. It was a good job his mother had never met this woman.

"Came in stinking to my bed and sent the rest of the night farting and grunting like a pig. And you want to know what's the matter? Jesus H. Christ!" She banged her cup down and glared at him defiantly.

So he'd had a few too many. He had already decided he was going to cut back, starting next week. And yes, he remembered throwing up, tasting the greasy grilled cheese sandwich he'd had earlier and which must have been to blame, but he thought he'd got it all in the sink. He couldn't believe he had given her the bruise, but he wasn't going to argue the point, not with the head he had on him.

Bishop was dressed for his weekly Sunday inspection of the camp. She had pressed his uniform and polished his boots to his uncompromising standards the day before. The pant creases were straight as knife blades, and the sun blazing through the window made mirrors of the glittering toe caps of his boots. He had shaved his cheeks until they glowed and carefully waxed the tips of his struggling handlebar mustache. He had clipped more off the left side to make it even. Nobody could say that Sergeant Major Jack Bishop did not know how to set an example. Only the reddened eyes and the terrible pounding behind them spoke of the abuse he had delivered to his body the night before, an endless line of glasses of navy rum chased by more than a gallon of beer.

He lifted his fork and pointed it at her, much in the manner that he raised his swagger stick and pointed it at prisoners and those beneath him in rank. "For a woman, you've got a dirty mouth," he said.

She closed her bathrobe around her tightly, collected her cup and saucer, and turned and walked to the door that led into the kitchen. "Fuck you," she said, as she closed the door behind her.

Bishop half rose from his chair. He'd knock the words back down her throat. He heard the slamming of the bedroom door and the clicking of the bolt, and concluded that the effort was more than he cared to expend. He would sort the bitch out later. He finished his coffee, stubbed out a cigarette in the remains of his breakfast, and got to his feet. He examined himself in the mirrored sideboard. He nodded, satisfied with what he saw. He checked his watch. He didn't usually conduct his weekly tour of the camp until early afternoon, but he wasn't about to hang around here until then, with the way things were. He would get it done now, then have the idle sods in the cookhouse find him a nice thick steak for his lunch, and some cold beers.

\- -

David patted his pants pocket and chuckled to himself as he approached the camp. Every few steps he broke into a trot, then slowed to a walk again. He doubted that Bishop would be around on a Sunday, and even if he was, David would keep out of his way. He wasn't really sure what the Germans would be doing. They wouldn't be working. Nobody worked on Sundays. He didn't know if they had a church, or even if they went to church, except for funerals like the one last week. He kicked a rock and watched it bounce into the tall grass at the side of the road.

\- -

Bishop stepped out of the orderly room and pulled at the brim of his cap, making it snug on his large head. He had always admired the way the military police wore their red caps low on their faces, hiding their eyes so that there was always some doubt about what might be going on in the minds underneath them. People really had to go out of their way to look you in the eye when the brim was well down, and most didn't choose to. He stamped his feet so that the tucked bottoms of his khaki trousers fell properly over the tops of his freshly blancoed gaiters. He checked his mustache and fitted his swagger stick neatly under his left arm. It was time. Bishop entered the compound through the gate held open by a Veterans Guard private and, as he did every Sunday morning, began his measured tour of the camp. It usually lasted thirty minutes and left him with the feeling that everything was right with the world. He grinned as he passed the cookhouse hut and the stacks of cordwood that the Kraut sailor had moved four times before the wood had finished back where it had originally been. That had been a long night for the fucker. If you wanted to play the old soldier, try playing it with Jack Bishop!

He arrived at the open area between the huts. A dozen prisoners, tanned and most of them wearing just PT shorts, several of them barefoot, were playing soccer on an abbreviated pitch, their shirts dropped on the ground to serve as goal posts. Bishop watched the game for a few minutes, and if he did think about the fact that his presence had anything to do with the play suddenly drifting to and remaining at the far side of the short pitch, he did so happily. When he moved on, the players spread out across the full pitch again.

At another clearing one of the POWs, a sergeant out of the German tank corps was pointing at a sheet of music resting on a finely crafted easel made by one of the prisoners. Bishop was constantly ordering him to get a haircut. The prisoner wore an Iron Cross decoration said to have been pinned on him by Hitler himself. They were good with their hands, with tools, Bishop grudgingly conceded. Three other POWs sat in front of the easel, paying close attention and nodding while the tank sergeant lectured them in German. Two of them had violins, the other a flute. The four of them, Bishop knew, had played in a full symphony orchestra when they were in the big camp at Lethbridge. And they had bought all their instruments from Eaton's Catalogue! Eaton's fucking Catalogue! A joke. A big fucking joke.

Eric Kruger sat on the steps leading up into the barracks hut that he shared with fifteen other prisoners. He had just listened to a radio report from the Canadian Broadcasting Corporation that suggested the Americans and British and their allies were pushing back a German military machine that was rapidly falling apart. It was no secret that several of the huts had homemade receivers and nobody, not even Bishop, seemed to worry about the infraction of camp rules. This attitude alone seemed to confirm for Kruger that the reports were probably accurate, that Hitler and his cohorts were being squeezed on all sides and that it was just a matter of time before the whole madness would be brought to an end, before he would be shipped back home, to whatever awaited him there.

A movement outside the perimeter fence, about twenty yards away from the rear of the hut caught his attention. He smiled when he saw a head of coppery hair above a young face poke through the tall grass. The boy, whose name he knew was David, frowned as he examined the stretch of fence and the huts beyond it.

Kruger was on his feet. He darted into the barracks hut, fumbled in the pocket of the tunic lying on his bed, transferred the contents to his shirt pocket, and left the hut by the rear door.

Kruger walked along the fence, searching the tall grass where he had seen the boy, noisily clearing his throat as he went. In a moment, the boy stepped out from the high grass, smiling shyly.

Kruger grinned at the boy. "Good morning." Nearby, a couple of POWs passed, smoking and talking quietly, along a bordering path. In the distance a Veterans Guard private paced along the fence on the other side of the camp.

"Hi," the boy said.

Kruger was close to the wire now, the boy just a couple of paces away on the other side of the fence.

"You are David, I think?" he said, and the boy quickly nodded in confirmation.

"David Evans," he said. "We were sorry about your friend, at the Jensens."

Eric nodded. "Yes, thank you. It is very kind of you to say that. And that was a very nice thing the people did for him, at the church."

The boy nodded, agreeing. He lifted one foot and used the toe of his shoe to scratch the back of his leg through his new flannels.

Eric noted the freshly polished shoes, and made a guess. "You have been to church, this morning?"

The boy nodded. "And this afternoon I have to go to Sunday school. So that's twice in one day."

Kruger laughed, a small happy laugh. "So, David Evans, that's a good name."

"It's Welsh."

"Ah, Welsh, of course. I know the Welsh." Eric nodded, and noted the look of surprise. "Let me see." Kruger searched his memory. "Ah, I know." And he recited, "Taffy was a Welshman, Taffy was a ... something."

"Thief!" David supplied, laughing, and he continued the verse:

Taffy came to my house, and stole a leg of beef.
I went to Taffy's house, but Taffy was in bed,
So I picked up the pee pot and hit him on the head.

"I remember now," Kruger laughed. "A funny rhyme."

"It is if you're not Welsh. My dad told it to me. But not when my grandad was there. He doesn't like it."

"Ah, I understand," Kruger said. "My name is Eric, Eric Kruger."

David's lips moved, shaping the name.

- -

At the far end of the path on which Kruger stood, about thirty yards distant, Bishop walked past the end of the path where it intersected with another one. His eyes were on a group of Germans at the far end of the camp, by the east fence. They were huddled together and might or might not be up to something that Bishop could find fault with. He stepped out of their line of vision, preparing to take a circuitous route and surprise them. As he did so his eye caught a figure standing at the south perimeter fence some distance away. He recognized the sailor, Kruger, and wondered what he was up to. Was he thinking of running? Where did he think he would he run to? Bishop blinked as he saw movement outside the wire. A kid. *Those bloody kids again!* He stepped quickly back, cut behind the row of huts that fronted onto the gravel, and began his approach along the cropped grass that ran up to the huts' rear walls.

-- --

A faint, familiar sound drifted through the hot, still air.

"Church bells," Kruger said, lifting his head. "That is like home." He watched as David crinkled his brow, as though considering the likelihood of German church bells. "But it would be earlier, there is a difference in the time."

"Eight hours, I know," David said.

"That is good! They teach you well in school."

David glanced down at his feet, then looked up at the German's face. "My dad's there," he said. "He's a prisoner—he was captured at Dieppe." He looked steadily into Kruger's eyes.

Kruger's gaze stayed on David as he digested the boy's statement. "The Canadians, they were very brave at Dieppe, I think. I know that many died there."

"Yes, a lot did."

"Then he is very lucky, your father. To be alive, I mean. And to have you here for him when he comes home. You and your mother."

"Maybe soon."

"I think you are right, David. I hope it is so." And as much to himself as to David, "I would like also to be at home."

"Do you get letters and stuff?"

Eric Kruger realized where the conversation was headed and decided that half the truth is sometimes better than all of it. And many of the men in Camp 10 did get letters. "Yes, sometimes, letters come."

"What happens if you get sick, when you're a prisoner?"

"Well, you see a doctor. That is in the rules."

"What else is in the rules?"

"Well, there is the mail, the letters and the ... boxes?"

"Parcels," David supplied. "With soap and candy and things?"

"Parcels, yes."

"We send them for my dad." He paused before adding, "Do you get photos as well?"

Kruger's heart turned over. "Oh, yes, photographs."

"Do they have the same rules in Germany?"

Kruger hesitated, then nodded. "I'm sure they do, David." He sought to change the topic. "So, what do you and your two friends do, with no school—when you are not annoying the Sergeant Major?"

David rolled his eyes and laughed. "Oh, we go to the Spook House and things."

"Spook house? What is a spook house?"

"Spooks, you know."

Eric shook his head, puzzled. "No, spooks?"

"Yeah, spooks!" David wiggled his hands in the air and moaned, "Whooooaaahhhhh ... spooks ... ghosts ... Whooooahhhhh!"

Kruger rocked back on his heels, laughing, "Ah, ghosts are spooks, I see! So a spook house is a ghost house, yes?"

"Right!" David seemed pleased.

"And where is this spook house?"

David told him, and told the Dorney story as well. "Then he hung himself with binder twine from the ceiling. He's supposed to walk around in there, so we go and listen."

"And have you heard him?"

"Well, yeah. Least, I think so. Ian said it was him."

"Ah, the redheaded one," Kruger said. "Then, if Ian said it was so." David laughed at the maybe-maybe-not note in the German's voice. They both knew Ian would say just about anything.

Kruger reached into his shirt pocket as they laughed and brought out the whistle he had crafted from a piece of willow twig. The length of the whistle had been carved in an intricate pattern of interweaving lines and shapes. He blew a short test blast on the whistle, then handed it through the wire to David, whose eyes lit up as he took it.

David dug his other hand into his trouser pocket and pulled out three cigarettes, a little worse for their journey, wrapped in a scrap of newspaper. "Great minds," David chuckled as he passed the cigarettes through the wire.

"Pardon?"

"What my mom always says when we do something at the same time," David explained. "Great minds think alike."

"Ah, I understand," Kruger said. He closed his hand around the cigarettes, and as he did, he saw a shadow cross the boy's face.

"No! Look out!" David shouted.

Bishop's swagger stick ripped through the air and struck the back of Kruger's hand. The German cried out at the stunning pain. He moaned and bent double, tucking the injured hand under his arm.

Bishop stood, vicious, lethal. His swagger stick was raised to strike again, but he lowered it, slowly, apparently satisfied that he had made his point. He prodded the German with the stick. "You're not going to learn, are you, Admiral?"

He placed the hobnailed sole of one gleaming boot on the cigarettes and ground them into shreds of paper and tobacco. He turned and glared through the wire at David's stricken face. He lunged suddenly, and David danced back as the snake-tongue tip of the swagger stick darted between the strands of wire, just missing him.

"Last warning," he said, pointing the stick at David. "You get yourself away from this fucking camp and you stay away! You hear?" Menacingly, he stepped close to the wire.

David was out of Bishop's reach, and he did not retreat. He held Bishop's stare.

Bishop said, "What are you, anyway, boy? Bloody simple, or something? Eh? Did they drop you on your head or something?"

David turned a worried face toward Kruger. The German remained bent over, protecting his damaged hand.

"Do you know what bastards like him are doing to your old man? Do you know what they do to prisoners in them Jerry prison camps? Do you?"

David lips trembled. He made a helpless gesture toward Kruger. The German's face was grey, and he groaned as he moved his hand. He looked up at David. "Go home, David," he said. "It is better that you go home."

David reached out a hand, as if he would touch the German through the wire. Bishop's swagger stick rose, poised.

David left his hand outstretched, just out of Bishop's reach.

Bishop turned on the German. "Get into your barracks." The simple instruction was laced with menace.

Bishop turned on David again, but before he could speak, David said, "You didn't have to do that." His eyes spilled tears. "You didn't have to hurt him. He wasn't doing anything wrong." He held the whistle up as evidence. "He was just giving me this. He hasn't done anything wrong!" David turned and began making his way through the tall grass. He turned once and watched as Bishop marched Kruger up the stairs of the barracks hut, his swagger stick pointed at the German's back.

David turned and trudged away, the stalks of dry grass brushing his arms. As he reached the edge of the road leading back to Willow Creek, he knuckled away a flow of tears.

"He didn't do anything wrong," he sobbed.

chapter twenty-three

Incident at Willow Creek:
Following the incident with the cigarettes, Warrant Officer Second Class
Jack Bishop paid a visit to Mrs. Evans, apparently to advise her of the visit
by her son to the camp to see the prisoner Kruger, and that her son should
be advised against any further such visits. Obviously Bishop's approach did
not achieve the result he had intended it to.

Liz Thomas looked up as her husband opened the door.

"We thought we might go for a walk," he said. "Up by the cathe-
dral. Want to come? What are you reading anyway?"

"No, you lot go," she said. "I just want to sit and think a while."
She tapped the pages in her hand. "Just some stuff mum had.
Doesn't make much sense, so far."

He walked over and kissed her forehead. "Okay. Love you."

"Love you," she replied.

She returned to the report. "The visit by her son ..." She shook
her head as if to clear her thoughts, but nothing was any clearer.
Which Mrs. Evans, for God's sake! Which son?

- -

As he stood before his mother, the details burst from David like
spillage from a breached dam.

"And then Bishop just, just," and David's hands mimed the
blow, "smashed, crashed the stick right down on his hand and it
must have hurt because he bent over and was trying not to cry but
he was crying, and he had his hand under here," and he tucked
his own hand under his arm to show her. "And Bishop stomped
the cigarettes all to bits on the path, and ... he really hurt him,
Mom."

She took his face in both hands and held it against her chest
while she wiped away his tears.

David described the rest, and Kristin's anger climbed.

"Then Bishop brought up about my dad and the Germans and
what they're doing to him because the camps there are bad places.
He doesn't know that, Mom, does he?"

Kristin pulled the dark tousled head closer. She thought of
Bishop, the vicious bastard, and she thought of Gareth, and what

indeed the Germans might be doing to him because who the hell really knew? A sudden, unbidden image flared in her mind, of herself spread out on the bed upstairs with Roper kneeling between her thighs. She shut it out and held her son tight.

"I wish I had some answers, sweetheart," she said softly. "I just don't know. I honestly don't know. I don't know about Bishop, or why he is like he is. I don't know about the Germans, and I don't know why it has to be us. And your dad, I just wish he was back here with us and all of this would go away."

She was sobbing as she finished, deep sobs that shook both of them as her frustration and anger overflowed. And along with these thoughts, a fear ran through her, like a stream of chilled water, a knowledge that she kept telling herself couldn't be true.

David felt his mother shaking, felt the sobs deep in her body, and her struggle to control them, which she finally did. He pushed Bishop out of his mind and patted his mother's hand. "It'll be all right, Mom," he said. "You'll see, it'll be all right." He found the words that seemed to be on the lips of all the adults. "They say it's going to be over soon anyway. Hitler's on the run."

Kristin's final sob turned into a weak laugh as David recited Henry Jensen's perpetual line. Poor bloody Henry. She lifted her apron and wiped her eyes. "I'm sure it will be, Davie. I'm sure you're right."

She looked down at him, forcing her tears back. "And anyway, I doubt that this Eric Kruger is to blame for any of it, any more than your dad is."

David nodded his head in firm agreement.

"I'm sure he would rather be somewhere else," she said.

"That's for sure! At home, I bet!"

Kristin laughed and agreed. "But, Davie. I really think you should stop going near the camp. It worries me, what might happen. It seems there's nothing but trouble comes out of there."

"But Mom, Eric needs a friend! He really does." He added, "I'm his friend, Mom. I have to be."

"Oh God, Davie—"

"No! Listen, Mom, what if my dad needed a friend? We would want him to have one, wouldn't we? If there was somebody like me?"

The dark, wide eyes pleaded for her understanding. Kristin sighed, knowing she was beaten. He was the double of his father when it came to latching on to any stray that came by. An elevated sense of personal responsibility that many would call misplaced, she had told Gareth. It was the quality in both of them that she loved the best, and the one that could drive her to distraction. Always so reasoned, always so ... right. It was why Gareth was where he was today instead of safe at home, safe in their bed.

She nodded, slowly. "Yes, sweetheart, we would want that. Of course we would." She looked at the clear-eyed, smiling young soldier in the photograph on the sideboard. "I hope he has a friend," she said, and thought, dear God, let him have a friend. "But I want you to promise you'll keep out of Bishop's way," she said. "He is a bad piece of business."

- -

Bishop followed the submariner into the barracks hut after watching the Evans kid retreat.

The German stood by his cot, the injured hand cradled in his other hand. Bishop stopped in front of him and the German's eyes came up to meet his.

"You are thick," Bishop said, a pause between each word. "You know that?"

The German made no reply.

"Thick as three short planks," Bishop said. "You have a cushy billet, you and your fuckin' Nazi friends. And what do you do? You shit in it? Don't you?" He shook his head. "Thick."

Eric Kruger said nothing, waiting for the rest.

"Fraternizing," Bishop said. "That's what you were doing out there. And fraternizing, my friend, is not allowed."

"Some men work outside," Kruger said, quietly. "They are with people all the time."

"Don't talk back to me," Bishop snarled. "Now, let me see." He assumed a thoughtful pose, an elbow resting in the opposite palm, forefinger against his cheek, the swagger stick dangling from his hand.

"Let me see, you can't use heavy tools right now, I would think, what with your sore hand." He laughed. "So, right. Get your toothbrush."

Eric Kruger was puzzled. "Toothbrush?"

"You suddenly deaf as well? Get your fuckin' toothbrush and come with me."

The German turned to his locker and picked his frayed toothbrush from his tin mug. He followed Bishop as he marched out of the hut to the communal latrine and bath hut.

Bishop ordered the two prisoners on latrine duty out of the building. He pointed Kruger to the first of a row of six porcelain toilet bowls, separated from each other by a low half-wall of plywood.

"Clean them," he said, nodding to the toilets and to the toothbrush in Eric's uninjured hand. "When I get back I want to see these piss pots shining like the Northern Lights." He paused. "Is that clear?"

"I understand."

"Good. Well get at it. I have some business to attend to, with your young friend's mother."

Concern showed on the German's face.

Bishop smiled. "I'll bet you'd like to carve something for her, wouldn't you?"

The German made no reply, but got to his knees and started scrubbing the sides of the first of the dingy toilet bowls.

"She'd blow it for you as well, I wouldn't be surprised." He turned and left.

Kruger looked down the line of toilet bowls. He took a deep breath, let it go in a long sigh, and applied the frayed bristles to the brown stains that rimmed the toilet.

- -

David heard the motorbike in the distance, coming closer. He was sitting by the window in the front room, reading a two-day-old copy of the *Lethbridge Herald*. In it was a list of soldiers killed in action. One corporal had been killed accidentally. It seemed queer to go off to fight in a war and get killed in an accident. He wondered if the corporal had got run over, like John Thompson. There was a list of men "missing" from the Alberta Regiment. David hoped somebody found them all before the Germans did.

The motorbike engine was louder now, approaching down the main road.

There was a report in the paper that he had asked his mom about, a couple of the words he wasn't sure of.

NEW YORK (A.P.) The Berlin Home radio said today, "The would-be perpetrators of Hitler's assassination have escaped, but the police were on their trail."

Some people had tried to kill Hitler—some other Germans. "Too bad they missed," his mom said. And another report said that the Allies were within twelve miles of Paris. His mom said that sounded like good news, like our side was starting to really win. Maybe his dad would be home and wouldn't need one of the Christmas parcels described in another report. David had clipped the report. He wasn't sure why his mother had snorted a couple of times when she read it out loud at his request.

"This is what your dad should be getting." She had stressed the "should" so he hoped she was right. She read aloud: "Enamel dish, cutlery, face and dishcloths, soap, shaving stick, toothbrush and powder, and a Christmas dinner of canned chicken, maple butter, and plum pudding.

"'Lieutenant Eva Closeman of Montreal said, 'Cheerful colours were selected for the dishes, plate, cup, saucer, and bowl for psychological reasons.'" This is where his mom had snorted, but when he asked, "What?" she just shook her head and read on. "'The dishes not only brighten meals for Canadians but in many cases replace articles they have had to improvise due to shortages in Germany.'" She had muttered "Jesus!" at that. "'The tin of maple butter was chosen for its Canadian atmosphere.'"

His mother had laughed. "Right," she said. "And then we'll have a nice weekend at the Banff Springs Hotel," which David didn't understand at all, and his mom didn't bother explaining.

David looked up as the motorbike engine revved then stuttered to a stop. He drew back the lace curtain, caught his breath, and quickly dropped it back into place. "Mom!"

"What?" He heard the clatter of dishes. "I'm busy, David."

"It's Bishop! Its Bishop! He's here!"

Sergeant Major Bishop, pressed and polished, was making his way up the front path. His boots thudded across the porch boards. The door bell made its low buzzing-rattling sound.

David's mom came out of the kitchen, wiping her hands on a dish towel. The bell buzzed again. She took her apron off over her head, tossing it onto the floor, and brushed her hands through her hair. She wouldn't have tossed the apron onto the floor if she was going to invite Bishop inside. David noted this with relief.

Kristin opened the door and faced Jack Bishop. She nodded a neutral greeting. She could smell his sour body sweat across the small space between them. He's enjoying this, was her first thought as Bishop returned her nod and rocked his body slightly, officiously, on the balls of his feet. His polished boots creaked as he moved.

"Mrs. Evans?"

Kristin nodded. "That's right." As if he had needed to ask.

His eyes flicked from her face down to her breasts, and she involuntarily folded her arms across her chest. A defiant move more so than defensive, one which raised Bishop's eyebrows a fraction.

"Ah, your lad," he said.

"David," Kristin said. "What about him?"

Her brusqueness clearly was not what Bishop had expected, and he seemed briefly lost. He cleared his throat and said, "Well, ah, we have a bit of a problem."

Kristin let the statement sit in the afternoon heat. Bishop was standing directly in the mid-afternoon sun, acutely conscious of the sweat rolling down into the pads of flesh that encased his neck. If Kristin Evans was aware of his growing discomfort, she showed no concern for it.

"He's been running after the Jerries," Bishop announced, as though delivering news of a battlefield death.

She frowned, as if needing time to digest the information. "Running after them?" she said, as if the words needed decoding.

Bishop shuffled uncomfortably. It was not supposed to be this difficult, the way he had envisioned it. And the sun was a killer. He cut to the chase. "He seems to have become, ah, friendly with one of them." Now it was as if he were announcing an allied victory. "He's been bringing him cigarettes!"

Kristin nodded pleasantly. "Yes, so I understand."

Bishop started, then stared at her. *Had she heard what he said?* He cleared his throat. He realized that his hesitation was beginning to lose him the initiative. She coolly waited and said nothing.

In fact, he realized, from the second she had opened the door, he had not had the initiative. "What I thought was," he said, pushing out his chest, "I thought that we, you and me, could have a chat about the problem, like, a little talk, so to speak?"

Bishop grappled for some measure of control as his cheeks took on a deepening shade of red. Kristin thought, this is the big bad Sergeant Major Bishop? She recalled what Steve Roper had said about him: "He doesn't know how to stop, once he gets started. Just digs the hole deeper and deeper." A smile flickered across her face, and was gone.

Bishop misjudged the smile, thinking he had finally hit the right note. His eyes fell again to her bosom. "I thought that maybe, the boy, well, that I could ..."

Her face was without expression as Bishop blundered on.

"You know, maybe give him a quarter, to get some ice cream ... " The sweat dripped down his face now, from under his sodden hat band, onto his cheeks and off their folds into the creases around his mouth, and off the end of his nose.

Kristin kept her arms folded across her chest, and let him sweat. He seemed to have run out of words. She smiled. "And what then, Mr. Bishop?" she said. "What if we send him for ice cream?" And again Bishop misjudged her tone. His eyes took on a sly light, and he chuckled and opened his mouth to speak, but she spoke first. "But we know what then, don't we?"

Bishop frowned, confused. The words were right, but the message wasn't. And it didn't get any better.

"Just you and me, Mr. Bishop? Nice and cozy? Was that the idea?"

Bishop's eyes darted away then back to her face. He could read the smile clearly now, as she continued.

"You know, the Americans and the Aussies have it all over you. At least when they proposition a woman they offer silk stockings and decent liquor. They do it nicely." She dropped the smile. "And they've never used my son as a threat."

She unfolded her arms and straightened up. "I don't want you here, Sergeant Major." She made the rank sound like an affliction. "I don't want you here with your talk about my son, or with anything else for that matter." She jabbed a finger at him, forcing him to take a step backwards.

"And if he is making a friend there as you say he is, well, better that friend than a hell of a lot of others I could name." She dropped her pointing finger. "Goodbye, Mr. Bishop." She shut the door firmly in his face.

David had heard most of the conversation. While he wasn't certain what a proposition was, Ian had told him enough about his various uncles bringing silk stockings for his mom, and what they expected for them. But that was Ian's mom. David felt a swelling of pride for his mom. Boy, had she put Bishop in his place! He followed her as she walked back to the kitchen, where she started putting pans and dishes into the sink.

"What did he say?"

"You heard him," she said. "He has a problem with you going out there." She rattled a dish in the sink. "That's not all he's got a problem with," she muttered, and seemed to be saying it more to herself than to David. She shook crumbs from a dishcloth into the sink. "I must say that Ian has him dead to rights," she said, as she turned back to the sink. "Sergeant Major Asshole it is."

David hooted, then they both stopped and listened as the motorbike jumped to life out on the road. There was the sound of a crashing gear-shift, the roaring departure of the motorbike.

"Keep out of his way," Kristin said, and she went back to washing dishes.

She reminded him of that at lunch time the next day.

"You'll be out of his way after tomorrow anyway. Got the rodeo and everything coming up and then—ta-daaaa! —school!" She pirouetted twice and came to a dramatic stop, like a Spanish dancer, and David gave her a standing ovation.

The rodeo was going to be in Lethbridge on the coming Labour Day weekend, before school started on the Tuesday. Ian's mom had agreed to look after the store and the gas pump for the few days they would be away starting tomorrow, when his grandad Morgan was coming to take them to Lethbridge to stay the rest of the week.

"Did you say Ian was coming over before we go?" Kristin asked.

"He should be here any minute."

"Right then," Kristin said, and she turned to check the clock on the sideboard. "It's quarter to one. I have some shopping and a little visiting to do, get a little gift for your grandma, so I'll be back around four. Okay? Are you listening?"

"Four o'clock," David said.

"Don't go far, remember? You have to have a bath and get an early night. We're going to be up early tomorrow."

"Okay," David said. "Mom?"

"What?"

"Do we *have* to go to Lethbridge?"

"Yes, we do."

She was not looking forward to seeing Morgan Evans, who had not been back to Willow Creek since she had thrown the cans at him and ordered him out. If Morgan had been the only question, she wouldn't have gone near Lethbridge. But there was Olwyn and the rest of the family, and she wasn't going to deprive David of them, nor them of him. She was also going to be glad to put some distance between herself and Steve Roper. She had slipped once, but there would be no repeating.

"Anyway, you know how much you like the rodeo," Kristin said. "You wouldn't want to miss that."

That was true enough, David thought. For one thing, it was about the only time of year you ever saw the Indians off the reserves—and they usually won everything in sight. Even the boys David's age had long black hair down to their shoulders and wore old felt hats and rode their ponies bareback.

But it was for a whole week. He kept thinking about Eric Kruger, and Bishop.

His mom bent down and kissed him, and he looked up in surprise. She was only going shopping.

"Don't go far," she said

"Yeah, I know, I know."

chapter twenty-four

Incident at Willow Creek:
It is possible that a sudden change in Sgt. Major Bishop's domestic life that final day had put him in a mood that could have aggravated the situation that led to the four deaths. This is noted not in any way to excuse Bishop's extreme behaviour on that day, but simply to assist in understanding factors contributing to the events.

Liz Thomas stared at the words. *Four deaths*?

THURSDAY, AUGUST 30, 1944

Steve Roper was sure of just two things. First, Joe Kenny had gone. Vamoosed. He would turn up somewhere, eventually, and the army more than likely would catch up with him and he would be in shit up to his eyebrows. But he was gone. His room at the billet house was cleaned out, his single cardboard suitcase missing from its spot under the bed.

Second, Sergeant Major Jack Bishop was missing a wife. That seemed certain. Bishop had shown up that morning wearing yesterday's shirt, wrinkled and sweat-marked, and his uniform pants were unpressed. Of course, Helen Bishop could be sick, although whether she would ever have been sick enough to have been excused from her laundry and ironing duties was unlikely. The situation became even clearer when a corporal from the airbase to the east arrived with an invitation, and a request for an immediate RSVP, for Sergeant Major and Mrs. Bishop to attend a cocktail party that evening at the officers' mess, something to do with a suddenly received notice of a change of command. The Bishops were being included because of the many times the sergeant major had hastened to satisfy the base commander's wishes for certain work to be done, by supplying Germans for the labour. And such an invitation of course was also less an invitation than a firm order.

"I'll be there," Bishop told the corporal.

"And Mrs. Bishop, sir?"

"She won't be."

"She's ill, sir?" the corporal persisted.

"She's away," Bishop said. "Now fuck off."

Ordinarily he would not have spoken to a wing commander's emissary like that.

"I'll give the wing commander your message, sir," the corporal said dryly, and he was out the door of the orderly office and into his Jeep without another word.

"What do you want?" Bishop snarled as Roper stepped into the room. He had overheard the exchange with the visiting air force corporal. "I thought you were supposed to be on the job an hour ago."

"Man missing, sir," Roper said. "Private Kenny did not report for duty this morning."

Bishop scowled. "The useless prick'll be hungover. Go and drag him out, I don't give a shit what shape he's in."

Roper shook his head. "He's gone. I checked. Everything's gone, suitcase, the lot."

Roper had put the two missing persons together with no trouble at all. But then he had an advantage over Bishop. He'd been privy to Joe Kenny's vivid descriptions of his relations with Mrs. Bishop at every opportunity. He'd also heard about Bishop's inadequacies in the same department.

He watched as Bishop's mind turned, possibly connecting the missing Kenny with the absent Mrs. Bishop. He seemed suspicious but was perhaps not yet convinced that one and one might amount to two.

"I need another man," Roper said. "We're fencing again at the Oldman River."

Bishop barely heard him. He waved Roper to get on with things and stepped out onto the porch, deep in thought.

Roper picked a new VGC private, Arthur Harris, and twelve Germans, including Eric Kruger and Dieter Schiller. They loaded the trucks with tools and materials, and ten minutes later had arrived at an escarpment overlooking the Oldman River, just west of Willow Creek. The job, expected to take about a week, was to fence in a staked area the army had leased for vehicle storage. It seemed to Roper that the area was a long way from anywhere connected with the Canadian military. But he also knew, and was deeply grateful for the fact, that the organizing of military logistics was not always a product of the nation's finest minds.

It was Roper's practice to let the army keep cocking up, and to profit handsomely from the outcome. Today, he had made sure that twice as many fence posts and rolls of wire as were necessary had been loaded and delivered to the site. At the end of each work day Roper planned to return to the site and begin distribution of the excess materials to chosen customers, at a price that would at the same time please them and add to Roper's wartime profit.

With the money from almost a year of redistributing the army's wealth, Roper had already made down payments on three houses between Willow Creek and the airbase. The housing officers were happy to throw money at anyone with as much as a chicken coop to rent. They were constantly searching for accommodation for the endless flow of Commonwealth trainee flight crews. The knowledge that many of his tenants would eventually go on to meet horrific deaths in the skies over Europe did nothing to lessen Roper's determination to gouge every nickel he could from the situation. Roper had been sent in as cannon fodder himself, and had come back. And nobody had said much in the way of thanks. The idea of becoming a landlord had grown out of some overheard conversations in the beer parlour at the Willow Creek Hotel, with small-time farmers bragging about how much the military was paying in rent for broken-down shacks.

The route to becoming a property owner had become clear after a couple of the same farmers mentioned that they wouldn't mind a few sheets of plywood, if he had some extra, you know. If he could manage to give them a couple of Jerries off his road crew, to finish up a job for a couple of days, there would be a coupla bucks in it for him. The coupla bucks had quickly become enough for him to make the down payments on the houses, and the rents he received from the military more than covered the mortgage payments. Not only that, but Roper soon realized that he could upgrade the houses by claiming exaggerated costs for repairs and damages as the trainees completed their courses and were shipped off to Europe. As long as he filled in the forms, the government kept paying up.

The houses were in better condition now than when he had bought them. And the better shape the houses were in, the more rent he could demand, like a kind of perpetual-motion money machine, he told himself. Roper hoped the war would keep right on going. Nor was he the only one helping himself. He knew one major in Lethbridge who every morning signed out a crew of German prisoner tradesmen from the camp and put them to work on a row of six new houses he was putting up on land he had bought cheap. The only significant difference between the two projects, apart from the major's supply of gall, was that the major had not been caught in the act by Sergeant Major Jack Bishop.

It had happened early in the spring, when Roper was on one of his supply runs, this time with a load of blankets and cases of canned meats. He'd acquired them from the quartermaster's stores in Lethbridge through the usual combination of sheer brazenness and requisition forms authentically stamped and signed with a scrawled name that could have been anyone's. All that mattered to the harassed stores sergeant was that he had the pieces of paper that showed the stuff had been moved under proper authority. Roper brought the supplies back to Willow Creek on a Friday night, preparatory to a sales run to the Pincher Creek area the next day. It was then that he'd run into Bishop, who should have been well away from the camp and into his Friday night piss-up.

Roper rolled through the camp gates and Bishop flagged him down. His gut clenched as he leaned through the truck window. "Sarn't Major," he acknowledged.

"Corporal Roper. What's this? I thought you were off duty?"

"I am, sir. I just thought I'd give the truck a checkout. It's been running a bit rough the last few days."

Bishop nodded. "Very thoughtful, corporal."

Roper didn't reply.

"What you got in the back?" Bishop nodded to the rear of the truck where the side and back canvasses had been put in place, closing in the deck.

"Dunno, sir; I never looked."

Bishop smiled. "What's say we have a look."

Roper sighed and climbed down out of the cab. Visions of a jail cell rose in his mind.

Bishop pulled back the canvas tail-flaps and climbed up into the truck. Roper heard him fumbling around, moving boxes, and then Bishop was standing at the open flaps, grinning down at Roper. He climbed down and dusted off his uniform pants.

"Carry on, Corporal," he said.

Roper stared at him. "Sir?"

"I said, carry on."

There was no question that the stuff inside the truck should not have been there, and no doubt that Bishop knew that. Roper's first thought was that Bishop wanted some of the action, and he ventured, "Ah, sir, we—"

Bishop's raised hand stopped him. "I said carry on, Corporal. I think we understand each other."

And it became clear what he meant. Bishop wanted no interference in the running of his camp. Roper was the next-senior NCO, and had been the only one to raise any kind of objection to some of Bishop's primitive treatment of the prisoners. Those objections had since ceased, with the exception of Roper's spontaneous intercession in the business with the young pilot, Schiller. Bishop could still fuck him up on that one, as he had made clear afterwards.

"Just watch yourself, Corporal," he had said, and the fact that he had said it casually, with none of the usual bombast, was warning enough. Roper would watch himself.

Roper's increasing cash supply bought him young attractive women in whatever community he decided to visit. Sometimes it was Lethbridge and occasionally he got up to Calgary. He had come to know what it must be like to be an American in uniform, with money.

He had thought he had struck gold with Kristin Evans, and that his sexual needs were settled for the duration of the war. But his hopes had been flattened a few days after their one memorable encounter, when he pulled in at the gas pump near closing time and asked her when David would be staying over at Ian's again.

"He won't be," Kristin said. "Not again. Not at all." They were alone, and she squared up to him. "I made a mistake," she said. "Just once. And I won't be making it again. That's it."

With the look on her face, and her posture, Roper recognized it as one of those times when you gracefully threw in your cards and left the table. He shrugged and smiled. "Well, everybody's allowed one," he said, and laughed as he saw her surprise that he wasn't going to push it. "And don't worry," he said. "I do not kiss and tell. Okay? Our secret."

Relief was in her face as she realized he meant what he said. "Right," she said. "Thanks for that. It means everything."

– –

Now Roper sat on the step of the five-ton truck, the door open to provide some shade from the fireball that was the late-morning sun. Shit, it was hot. And muggy. He searched the sky, but it was clear, just the faint smudge of a cloud line away to the south. He stood and called out, "Okay, lads, take a break, chow time."

As one, the Germans dropped their tools, wiping sweat from their faces. A couple of them had removed their shirts. Although they had already gained a dark tan during the summer, the day's searing heat had burned them.

The new Veterans Guard private, Harris, had found shade under a cottonwood tree some distance away, on the edge of the escarpment that ran down to the Oldman River. It looked as if Harris might have fallen asleep. Well, nobody was going anywhere.

"How's it goin', Eric?" Roper asked as the submariner approached the truck. Schiller, the young pilot, had also joined them. He was supposed to be over the flu but he still looked awfully pale, Roper thought. He had begged to be included in the fencing crew, rather than be left in the camp.

"It's all right," Kruger replied. "Not bad."

"Bishop still on your back, is he?" Roper had been away on a forty-eight-hour pass, checking on his business interests and keeping his line of supplies open. He had heard about young David's visit the day before, and its results.

"I try to stay away from him, but it is not easy. "

Roper nodded his sympathy. "Yeah, I know. Here." He slid a brown cardboard box to the tailgate of the truck. "Lunch! Come and get it boys!" The box was filled with sandwiches packed by the kitchen staff.

The men first lined up at the twenty-gallon water bucket on the backboard and waited their turn with the dipper. Roper had kept the barrel topped up with ice from an insulated box. Another twenty-gallon barrel sat under wet burlap.

Kruger rummaged among the sandwiches.

"Anything special?" Roper said. "Little caviar, maybe?"

"Cheese," he said.

"Well, that's a nice change," Roper said brightly, and Kruger laughed. Whatever cheese was, it was not a change.

"A cold beer would be nice with it, I think," Kruger said.

"I know, but there's a war on," Roper said darkly.

"I heard about that."

Roper sipped cold tea from a flask and he and the sailor watched the others seek patches of shade, some of them stretching out and closing their eyes.

"What is it about Bishop?" Kruger said. "Not just with me, but ... "

"He's a horse's ass," Roper said. "But don't quote me."

"Yes, the horse's ass, I know. But what makes him like that? Is it the last war? Was he a prisoner?"

"Prisoner?" He shook his head. "No, they'd have needed a long rope to yard that one in, son." He thought for a second, and added, "No, what you have in the Sergeant Major is your basic blue-ribbon prick. He was in the last war, yes, but he sat on his ass in the Canadian Training Division offices in England, totting up pay lists while the rest of us, our lads and yours, were being shot to ratshit and put six feet under."

The German nodded that he understood, and Roper continued.

"He had a brother that caught it, somewhere, I forget, maybe Vimy." Roper's face hardened. "Vimy, Jesus." His eyes drifted.

"You were at Vimy?" the German said, and the question brought Roper's focus back.

"Yeah, I was there. Shit-scared and seventeen years old." His thoughts drifted again. "Know what I remember about Vimy?"

The German shook his head, waiting, and Roper laughed. "I went to sleep one time with my groundsheet under me and it was lumpy as hell, the ground, lumpy, you know? Well, when the sergeant came and kicked us awake, I rolled my groundsheet up and I had been sleeping on one of your guys. Poor bugger was in pieces, and mostly under the mud, and the lump I had been feeling in the night? Well, that was his head."

Kruger had stopped eating as he listened to Roper's matter-of-fact description of the horrors of the Great War trenches.

"Know what I remember thinking? I kept thinking, there's no smell. Here was these poor buggers, your lot, dead and rotting in the mud, and there was no smell." He laughed.

"And then I figured it out. The fact is that the smell of death was the *only* smell! Everywhere, we were in it all the time. I could have had my nose in his face and I wouldn't have known any different." He sipped from his flask of tea. "That was Vimy."

Silence sat between them for a moment. Roper broke it.

"But we were talking about Bishop, weren't we." He hawked up some phlegm and spat it into the dust. "Thing about him, the thing to remember, is that he was nothing before this lot—your war—started. Nothing at all. He was clerking in a feedstore when they started hiring for the Guard. And when this is over, he'll be nothing all over again. Sitting behind a counter, taking shit from people."

Kruger nodded, following Roper's words.

"But right now, he's got the chance to make his mark. Everybody wants to leave a mark, something that says they were here. Bishop's brother made a mark. But Bishop's not made of the stuff his brother was. Inside the wire is the only place *he* can make his mark. There he has power, and power—as I'm sure you have noticed among your own people—does funny things."

"Yes, Steve, I had noticed," he said, and raised his hand halfway in a mock-Nazi salute.

"Right," Roper said. "Well, Bishop is going to make the most of it while he has it. It's that simple."

And it's not going to improve his mood any when by now he must have worked out that all the time Joe Kenny was bragging in the Willow Creek Hotel beer parlour about all the tail he was getting, he was getting it in Bishop's bed.

chapter twenty-five

Liz Thomas scanned the last page of the report.

Incident at Willow Creek:
The step-by-step events of that day have been reviewed as best we could
largely from the testimony of Cpl. Steve Roper, the boy Pauli Aiello, and
the few Germans who were willing to recall how the situation got started.

"You're gonna get shit, Davie," Ian warned as they wheeled their
bikes out onto the road. "Your mom told us to stay here and look
after the place."

David threw his leg over the bicycle seat and put his right foot
up ready on the pedal. "She's not coming back 'til four o'clock.
She said so."

Ian looked doubtful and David laughed. "I'm just gonna go and
see him before we take off for Lethbridge. They're over at the Oldman River. It'll only take us ten minutes."

Ian shook his head. "Jeez, Davie."

Kristin had warned Ian as she left, "You remember, Ian, don't
be roaming off anywhere. He's all ready to go away tomorrow. You
too, Pauli," she had added, and Pauli turned away.

"What's the matter? You scared of Bishop?"

Ian's face flushed and he rose to the challenge. "All I said was
that you'd get shit," he said. "And anyway, no. Who would be
scared of that asshole?"

"Come on," David said, and pushed off, sending the bike wob-
bling out onto the road.

"Come on!" he yelled, and gave an Indian war whoop. He shot
out onto the road, followed by Pauli riding a bike borrowed from
his sister.

David put his head down and pumped the pedals as hard as he
could. His mom would never know they'd been away.

- -

It was an hour after the prisoners had finished their lunch break
and returned to work when Steve Roper saw the three bikes bob-
bling along the highway toward them.

He chuckled, watching David spray pebbles as he braked and

turned his bike off the road, jumping out of the way to avoid Ian who raced in on his tail. Pauli was struggling along fifty yards behind, his chubby face crimson with the effort of trying to keep up.

"Well, if it isn't Lance-Corporal Evans and Private Mackenzie," Roper said. "Oh, and the other one," he added, as Pauli dropped his bike beside the other two.

Roper caught Kruger's questioning look and nodded permission. The German dropped the string-line he had been adjusting with the help of Schiller and walked over to the boys.

"Hello, David," he smiled. "How are you today?" He reached out and offered a hand. David could see the welts left by Bishop's stick.

"Wow," Ian said.

Eric withdrew his hand, embarrassed. "It is all right," he said.

"I brought some pop," David said, unbuckling the straps on a canvas pouch behind the seat of his bike. He undid some newspaper wrapping and brought out two bottles of Orange Crush. "You want some?"

Kruger queried Roper with his eyes, and Roper grinned and nodded. "Five-minute breather, grab a drink," he said, loud enough for the rest of the work force to hear. Roper scanned the highway. He had an uninterrupted view for about a hundred yards each way.

A sudden, swirling hot breeze stirred the grass and brought down some already yellowing leaves from the surrounding cottonwoods. Early fall, sign of a bad winter. Roper squinted off to the south, where the wedge of black cloud had thickened on the horizon.

The other prisoners had put their tools down and now wandered over to see the three boys. Most of them remembered Ian's earlier performance outside the camp wire. Some tried to get him to do the Colonel Bogey March song again. One of them was trying to remember the words.

"Hitler, with only one ball," he sang, badly, and Pauli folded over laughing at the German's poor effort.

Ian seemed to be overwhelmed by the sudden nearness of the Germans, with no wire as a barrier, and his face flushed to match his carrot hair as the prisoners egged him on to sing.

Harris, the Veterans Guard private, left the shade of his cotton-wood and walked closer to the group to see what was happening. He looked nervous, seeing the three boys surrounded by laughing Germans. But he relaxed as he watched Roper, apparently at ease with the situation. Still, he stayed by the truck, fingering the webbing sling on his .303 Lee Enfield rifle. He glanced frequently at the growing cloud mass off to the south, where an occasional flicker of lightning skittered across its dark belly.

Kruger and David had moved away from the group and now sat on a stack of fence posts. David took a swallow from a bottle of Orange Crush and carefully wiped the round top before passing it to Kruger. He lifted the bottle and let the warm, fuzzy sweet drink run down his throat.

"Ah, that was so good," he said, carefully following the ritual of wiping the top before passing it back to David.

David reached out for the bottle, and his hand stopped at the same time as Kruger's did. The work site was silent. Bishop stood twenty feet from them. He had parked his Jeep below the steep dip in the highway and walked the rest of the way unnoticed.

He had said nothing, just let those prisoners closest to him realize that he was there, and watched as their laughter at the boys fell away. Like falling dominoes, the laughter had died, starting at the outside of the ring of prisoners surrounding Ian and Pauli, until it stopped at the centre.

Now Bishop said, "What's going on?" and the Germans fell back.

Kruger scrambled to his feet, and the movement attracted Bishop, who then saw David.

Bishop shook his head, slowly, deliberately. "I do not believe it." He stepped toward David, who jumped up from the pile of fence posts and backed away.

Ian and Pauli had scuttled away from their group of Germans and headed for their bikes. David saw them moving and ran in the same direction, the three of them arriving at their bicycles at the same time.

Ian said, "Let's go." He had his bike turned toward the highway and was in the saddle before anyone could argue with him.

Harris gripped his rifle tighter and his eyes darted back and forth between Bishop and Roper.

"There's no problem," Roper addressed Bishop, carefully. "The men were just going to take a drink break, and the kids showed up. They're on their way now." He jerked a thumb toward Ian and Pauli, already on the edge of the highway and David, his bike upright, a short distance from them.

Bishop glared at the boys, and turned a scowling face to Roper. "Get them back to work," he said, his hand sweeping around the clustered Germans. "And I'll take care of those three." He turned and aimed a finger at the three boys. "Get moving. Now."

Ian whispered to David, "Come on, Davie." Pauli wheeled his bike past both of them, ready to pedal.

David looked at Ian, then back at Bishop. "We're on the road," he said to Bishop. "We can be here and you can't stop us. It's not your road."

A snort of laughter escaped Roper and he threw a hand up to his mouth in a vain attempt to muffle it as Bishop's head shot round. Roper tried to recover, then shrugged, "The kid's right. They're on a public road." He saw the look in Bishop's eyes. "Anyway, it's my fault, if it's anybody's. I let them on the site."

Bishop's mouth curled. "I think there's a lot of things that are your fault, mister." He pointed a finger at Roper. "And I'm going to fix that." He nodded, confirming the promise. "All the trouble I've had seems to come when you're around, you know that?"

The accusation made no sense, but Bishop was not engaging in rational debate. He was in search of a target. "I'm going to open the book on you, Corporal," he said. "The whole fucking book."

He swirled suddenly, at a movement among the Germans, who had all been locked in place, watching the confrontation and glad for once that it was not one of them on the receiving end of the Sergeant Major's fury.

Dieter Schiller had stepped up to the truck and was in the act of filling the water dipper from the drum on the tailgate. He was streaming with perspiration, wiping his brow with a shirtsleeve.

"Put that down!" Bishop's voice cracked out, and the young prisoner stopped, his hand holding the dipper just above the surface of the cool water and the floating pieces of ice.

"Put it down," Bishop repeated.

The German looked at the dipper in his hand, at the ice fleck-ing the water in front of him. He turned to Bishop and said, plain-tively, "*Ich bin durstig* ... *Ich* ... I need ... *trinke* ... a drink ... *bitte* ... please."

Bishop covered the short distance to Schiller in three quick steps and knocked the dipper from the German's hand with his swagger stick. The dipper fell into the water barrel, sending up a fountain of water, a few drops of which splashed the German's face.

"Get over there," Bishop ordered, pointing to where the rest of the Germans had huddled.

Just then, a flurry of rain spattered the site. The mass of cloud from the south had expanded and travelled quickly. Jagged cracks of lightning flickered across the bottom edge, and in the distance, thunder rumbled.

David automatically counted—one, two, three, four seconds between the flash of lighting and the thunder. That was supposed to be how many miles away, one per second, the storm was. The heated air felt like a blanket over them.

Schiller retreated before Bishop's towering anger. But his eyes went to the water barrel, and he licked his lips and wiped his forehead, which streamed with perspiration. "*Trinke*," he said, hoarsely, "A drink, *bitte*, please."

"Get back to work—" Bishop started, but Roper interrupted him.

"I did stop them for a drink break," Roper said. "They can't work in this heat without putting some fluid back. You know that."

Bishop turned to Roper, examining him for several seconds. Bishop nodded, slowly, and with a hint of a smile that put Roper's danger-senses on full alert, agreed.

"You're right, Corporal." He pointed his swagger stick at one of the prisoners at the edge of the huddle, a short, sandy-haired youth.

"You," he said, and pointed to the water barrel. "Get a drink."

The prisoner straightened up, looked warily at Bishop, then glanced at Roper. Roper nodded and indicated the barrel. "Go ahead," he said.

The German hesitated, looked once more at Bishop, and stepped over to the truck. He placed the scoop of the dipper in the bucket, raised it, and directed a stream of chilled water down his throat.

He sighed, a deep, satisfied sound, then quickly dipped again into the barrel and drank deeply once more. He turned and nodded to Bishop as he returned to the group. "Thank you," he said. Bishop ignored him.

David noticed the other Germans as the young man drank his fill. They had quickly shuffled into a line, anxious for a turn at the water barrel. Halfway down the line, Schiller wiped his face.

David glanced up as the day suddenly darkened. The sun had disappeared behind the solid mass of moving black cloud which had spread to almost fill the sky. The only daylight came from a thin band of brassy brightness to the north.

"Next man," Bishop said, and pointed to an older prisoner with greying hair at the head of the line. The German avoided Bishop's eyes as he stepped up to the truck and quickly satisfied his thirst and retreated.

"That storm's going to break," Roper said. "We should—"

"Shut up!" Bishop snapped, and pointed to the next German in line. "You."

David watched Kruger, who was standing behind his friend Schiller in the loose line the prisoners had formed. One more man went to the barrel, then Dieter Schiller stepped forward, his thirst etched on his face.

He took two paces and Bishop's hand rose like a policeman on traffic duty. "No, not you, Tinkerbell, you can wait." He gestured with his thumb. "Back of the line."

The German youth's face crumpled. He raised his hands as if praying. "A drink ... please."

Bishop grinned at him, and raised and pointed his swagger stick. "Back of the line," he said. "You went out of turn."

"Boy, what a jerk!" Ian was caught up in the event as though watching a movie, and his voice carried in the prickly, heated air. If Bishop heard it, he paid no attention.

Kruger spoke quietly to the pilot, and the young man, his shoulders drooping, nodded and stepped to the back of the line, behind his friend. Those in front of them drank until Kruger was next in line. Bishop pointed to him. "Admiral, yes, your turn."

As Kruger stepped forward, Schiller groaned and fell on one knee to the ground. Drops of sweat fell from his forehead and dappled the ground, and then there was a rush of bigger drops, summer rain, as a squall racing ahead of the main storm whipped through the site and passed on.

Kruger heard Schiller go down and he stopped and glanced behind him, then turned back quickly and stepped up to the water barrel. He drank a cup in two quick swallows, filled the dipper, and turned back toward his friend.

"Put it back."

Kruger stopped. "Sergeant Major, he is still sick, he needs water."

"Put it back."

David squeezed the rubber grips on his handlebars as he watched Bishop and the German.

Kruger wavered. He looked at the dipper of cold water held in his cupped hands. Schiller's raised eyes were fixed on him and Kruger took a step toward him with the water.

In a hoarse whisper, Roper, reading the light in Bishop's eyes, said, "Jesus, Eric, don't ... "

The German hesitated, then appealed to Bishop. "Please, Sergeant Major."

Bishop smiled. "Put it back."

A spattering of hail danced across the worksite and the last band of brassy sunlight dimmed under the enveloping cloud mass.

Kruger stood for just a second, before returning grim-faced to the huddle of prisoners.

Now Bishop turned his attention to the boys. He walked toward them, his face taut. Roper started moving in the same direction.

David held his ground as Bishop approached. A wind was building and David noted, oddly, that it seemed to be blowing in the opposite direction, from the north, to that of the ink-black clouds, which were flowing from the south. He wondered how that worked. A flash in the distance was followed by a snake-tongue flicker of lightning across the now totally black sky, and a bomb-like crash of thunder that shook them where they stood.

Bishop stopped in front of the boys and pointed his swagger stick.

"Get out of this area," he said, and he flinched as another crash of thunder obliterated his next words. A flying mix of rain and hail was peppering them now.

"Go!" Bishop thrashed the air with his swagger stick.

David shouted back, "It's not your road!"

"You little son of a whore!"

"Hey, that's enough!" Roper was at Bishop's side.

Bishop swung on him. "Fuck you, Corporal!" He laughed loudly. "We all know you're keeping it warm 'til her old man gets back—if he ever comes back!" He had raised his voice above the climbing wind for David's benefit.

"You asshole!" Roper yelled back.

"You're finished, mister!" Bishop bellowed. He had turned as he directed his threat at Roper, and now, looking across the short distance between them and the truck, he said, "Oh, you fucker!"

Schiller had scrambled to the truck and had the water dipper at his mouth. As he gulped and swallowed, water spilled down his face and onto the ground where it mixed with the hail that was now bouncing and rattling off the truck and piling up as white pebbles at his feet.

"You bastard!" Bishop ran toward the truck, his hand reaching for the holster on his belt, and the loaded revolver that sat there.

Kruger left the group of prisoners and started running to head-off Bishop while Roper moved to put himself between Bishop and Kruger, intending to stop the German.

David dropped his bike, hesitated, then chased blindly after Roper. "Eric!" he cried. "Eric!" and his voice was lost in a massive explosion of thunder and a barrage of hailstones that knocked the breath from his body and seemed to block out the entire world.

Bishop had his revolver in his hand and was two paces from Schiller, who had turned at the shouting and now stood, helpless. Bishop took the last step between them and raised the weapon, but as a club. He brought the barrel down on the young German's upturned face, just as Kruger hit Bishop with a diving tackle at knee height, bringing him crashing to the ground where they rolled in what was rapidly becoming a field of mud. The German scrambled on top of Bishop and fought to reach the revolver, which the collision had knocked from Bishop's grasp. Bishop brought a knee up and the German was thrown aside. Bishop was on his knees and also searching for the gun. The German threw a fist and Bishop gasped as the punch caught him below the ear and knocked him off balance again.

Roper had grabbed his rifle and stood on the edge of the struggle, poised and holding the weapon in both hands by its barrel, hoping to get a clean blow with the stock on either of the contestants, anything to bring it to a stop.

Roper yelled to Harris, the Guards private, whom the swiftness of events had left standing dithering and shifting from one foot to the other. "Watch them!" he shouted. Harris trained his rifle on the squad of Germans. Any who had had thoughts of joining the fray quickly decided against it.

Roper lunged with the butt end of the rifle, and as he did so his legs became entangled with Kruger's flailing legs. Roper went down, landing heavily, winded for a moment. He turned his head to see Kruger in control and straddling Bishop, who was on his back. The German had Bishop by the throat with his left hand, while his right held the heavy revolver. Before Roper could get a word out, the German brought the gun down in a swift arc and smashed it into Bishop's face, the end of the curved butt crushing into the hollow between the top of Bishop's nose and the corner of his right eye. There was a crunch of shattered bone and gristle, and Bishop screamed.

Roper staggered to his feet as Kruger lifted the gun and aimed another blow at Bishop's face.

"Eric!" Roper yelled, and he raised the muzzle of the .303 and pointed it at the German's face just two feet away. "Don't," Roper said, and the rifle flew from his hands and he was down again as David crashed with all the force his slight frame could muster into Roper's back.

"Davie! Davie!" Ian's terrified cry rose above the storm. Kruger halted the hand he had raised to strike again, and saw David sprawled on top of Roper, who was struggling to get back to his feet.

Roper and Kruger regained their feet at the same moment. Roper reached for the bolt on his rifle, and the German, still gasping from the struggle said, "Do not touch that, Steve." He held Bishop's revolver cocked, pointed at Roper's midsection. His eyes darted about the area, noting Harris frozen in position as he watched them.

"Eric, don't," Roper said. "This is not the way—"

"Put your gun down!" Kruger yelled at Harris, who looked helplessly at Roper.

Roper said, "Eric—"

"Tell him!" the German snapped.

Roper shrugged, nodded across to Harris. "Put it down," he said, and Harris lowered his rifle and laid it on the ground.

"Eric, listen, for Christ's sake—"

"No." The German shook his head. "It is too late."

"I'll tell them how it was," Roper persisted. "I'll tell them everything. Talk to him, David." He turned to where David stood. Ian was behind him, hypnotized by the events.

"Nobody will listen to you, Steve. You know Bishop is going to tell them about your ... business," he said with a crooked smile. He glanced down at Bishop, who gave a low groan.

"It will all happen again with him," the German said. "And much worse. "

The storm was delivering a hard driving rain now, limiting visibility to a few feet.

Roper raised a hand to reinforce his argument with the German. Suddenly, he was shouting, "No! No!" at Harris who had grabbed his rifle off the ground and was working the bolt frantically. Harris raised the rifle and fired even as Roper was yelling, "No!"

Kruger had swung to face Harris while Roper, realizing Harris' intent, had swept round on the boys and screamed, "Get down!" He saw Ian grab David as the rifle thundered, and both boys tumbled to the sodden ground.

As Harris rammed another cartridge into the breech, Kruger raised the revolver. The guard's rifle muzzle blossomed red and yellow flame, and the slug caught Eric Kruger in the left chest, high near the shoulder, and he staggered and fell. He struggled back to his feet and began a staggering, clumsy run toward the edge of the escarpment. He raised the revolver and squeezed the trigger as he stumbled toward a stand of trees. The wild slug from the revolver took Harris in the side of the head and blew shreds of brain onto a roll of fencing wire, where they clung while Arthur Harris flopped in the mud, his life seeping out in a crimson stream.

When the Veterans Guard private went down, Schiller ran forward, grabbed Harris' rifle, and ran after Kruger, who was just reaching the edge of the willows.

Across the clearing, David scrambled to his feet. He saw Kruger at the tree line, and he shouted, "Eric! Eric!" The German turned his head at the shout, and David gasped as he saw the injured man's chest. A dark mess that had nothing to do with the falling rain, stained his shirt.

He saw the young pilot now beside Kruger, and Kruger taking the rifle out of the younger man's hands and then waving him away, back to the others, and the pilot standing and watching as Kruger went from sight among the trees.

David's breath came and went in short, ragged bursts as he turned, bewildered, to Roper, whose face was creased into taut lines.

"What a fucking mess." Roper seemed to be talking to himself.

Ian was still on the ground. "Get up, Ian," David said, and he nudged him with his foot.

Ian laughed, a stupid, sputtering laugh, and David turned on him angrily. "Ian, get up!" He reached down to drag Ian to his feet, and Ian laughed the same stupid laugh again. But it wasn't a laugh. Ian was on his side, his eyes closed, still and quiet, except for the sound, a gurgle. Ian Mackenzie's final breath came out with a river of blood from the hole in his throat where Arthur Harris' first rifle shot had found its home.

David screamed, "Ian! Ian!" and jumped back. Roper knelt beside the body and groaned, "Oh, dear Christ!"

Roper swung around on one knee and surveyed the results of the day's work. Bishop lay near the truck, groaning. Harris' body was sprawled by the pile of fence posts. The Germans had emerged from cover and stood about, pale and shocked.

And then Roper saw someone running. "David? David!" he called. And again, louder, "David! Come back!" as he saw the boy's shape through the curtain of rain, disappearing, racing into the edge of the woods, where Roper had last seen Kruger.

chapter twenty-six

Incident at Willow Creek:
There was nothing from this point forward that was going to prevent
what happened.

Liz's hands shook as she reached for the letter from Moira and
read the rest:

> I looked after the graves like I said I would,
> before we moved here to Calgary. Willow
> Creek was finished, Kristin. When Rev. Warren
> left, nobody replaced him, and the church just
> stood empty and one night some kids playing
> with fireworks set it alight and it burned to the
> ground. Until we moved I took fresh flowers
> every week and Steve cut and trimmed the
> grass so neatly. It was always so pretty. We
> were among the last to leave Willow Creek,
> so there was nobody to look after the graves
> anymore. I went back once but I could hardly
> see the gravestones in the high grass. I started
> clearing it, but then I thought no, better to
> leave things as they are.

She read the next and final paragraph, then read it again, and
once more.

> I'm sending you this photograph of the graves as
> they were the day Steve and I left.
> With lots of love.
> Moira.

Liz dropped the letter and began scrabbling through the rest of
the papers, now scattered around her on the sofa. There were two
photographs, the family group and the wedding picture. She set
them aside and sifted through the letters, forcing herself to check

the papers one sheet at a time, then laying them to one side. She picked up the last loose page, laid it on top of the rest. The sofa was empty. Where was the photo of the graves. *Whose* graves? She shuffled the papers again. Maybe it had slipped behind the seat cushions. She lifted the two loose cushions. Nothing. As she bent to straighten the cushions, she saw the snapshot lying face down on the carpet, partly under the settee, where it had fallen. She turned it over. It showed two graves side by side, with identical gravestones. She couldn't make out the inscriptions. She went to the sideboard and retrieved a magnifying glass that she had been putting to use more and more lately on small-print items. She held it up to the photo and read the names on the gravestones.

\-\-

Moira Mackenzie stopped for gas just as Kristin returned from shopping and Kristin invited her in for a cup of tea.

"Those damn kids, I told them to stay around here," Kristin said as she poured tea.

"Ah, they probably found some shelter for a bit," Moira said. "They've got *that* many brains." She looked out the window. "It's easing up now, they'll be along in a minute." She took a pack of cigarettes from her purse. "Here, have a smoke."

Kristin waved the offer away. "No thanks, Moira."

"What, you quit?"

Kristin picked up the teapot and poured.

Moira's laugh was like water rushing over gravel. "Hey, only time that happened with me was when I got pregnant. Soon as I caught, I couldn't stand the thought of a cigarette."

Kristin handed Moira her tea.

"You're quiet. You okay?"

"Sure, just wondering where they can be."

Their heads lifted at the sound of sirens bursting into sudden wailing life from the direction of the POW camp. Kristin shivered and goosebumps prickled on her arms as the siren wailed, died, and wailed again.

Immediately in the siren's wake came the sounds of speeding vehicles approaching along the highway. The women reached the front porch just as three Jeeps, each carrying four uniformed soldiers armed with rifles, raced past the house. In the third Jeep

Kristin recognized Roper at the wheel. He glanced toward the house as the Jeeps flew past, and the look on his face sent a chill deep into her soul.

"David," she murmured.

- -

Eric Kruger leaned, gasping, against a cottonwood trunk. His senses reeled from the combined effects of the gunshot wound in his chest and the last twenty minutes of plunging through the thickets of trees and bush that overhung the banks of the Oldman River. Had he shot the guard? The man had gone down. The image blurred in Kruger's mind.

The blood was seeping slowly now from his wound. It was not pumping, so he guessed that no artery had been hit. But it leaked whenever he removed his hand from the wound. In the distance and through a wavering fog, he heard the rise and fall of the alarm siren. They used to laugh in the camp about the thing becoming rusty from disuse. It had never been turned on, other than for occasional tests, since the camp was built.

He had no plan, just the need to put distance between himself and Bishop. He should have killed him. He pushed himself away from the tree, and gasped as the wound opened. Blood ran down his chest and pain tore through him like a hot iron driven into flesh. He lurched through a patch of low bush and into a clear area facing a building, an old stone building, set low to the ground. He struggled to focus as the pain came in waves. His eyes cleared and he saw that the building's windows and doors were boarded over, the grass grown high against its walls. The place was abandoned. He sobbed with relief. He stared at the building and shook his head. Something ... then he laughed, a muffled, choking laugh cut off by a shaft of pain that dropped him to his knees. He breathed slowly, carefully, and climbed back to his feet. The place was surely David's Spook House; the boarded up doors and windows, and in the area that David had roughly described.

He edged along the wall under the sagging eaves until he came to a door. He pulled at two of the end boards and they gave way. He jammed the rifle barrel between the two boards and, gritting his teeth to prevent crying out at the fire in his chest, pried the boards so he could squeeze inside. He pulled the two boards together behind him, jammed them closed as well as he could, and stood still. He strained to make out shapes in the almost total darkness. A crack in the boards over a window at the far end of the room let in a sliver of light. He could see a flight of stairs in the middle of the room. He groped his way to the staircase and slowly felt his way up the steps. He was on a landing in a low-ceilinged room, almost an attic, he realized, as his head brushed a rafter. He put out a hand and felt the recess of a door. He pushed the door open, and made out the shape of the room. He staggered to the far end and eased himself into a corner. He placed his back against the wall, brought the rifle close, and closed his eyes. He slipped into unconsciousness as the haunting sound of the sirens rose and fell in his mind.

- -

"It wasn't his fault. It wasn't his fault," David sobbed as he pushed his way through patches of scrub willow.

"Eric?" he whispered as loudly as he dared. "Eric?" as he pushed on through the tangled undergrowth.

The eruption of violence at the work site was like some horrific nightmare. Eric smashing Bishop, who had started it all, and then the guard firing and the bullet hitting Eric with a sound like Mr. Wilson made when he chopped meat on his block in the butcher shop. And Ian, and that terrible noise he made that had sounded like a laugh. David rubbed his face hard, all over, as if that might somehow banish the images.

Suddenly, he stopped. He had been running through the bush without thinking of where he was going. Where was he? He looked around him. The river was behind him. Willow Creek and home were off to the south. He started walking again and within minutes his feet touched the hard surface of a path.

The words jumped into his mind.

"So, what do you and your two friends do with no school, when you are not annoying the Sergeant Major?"

"Oh, we go to the Spook House and things. "

"Spook house? What is a spook house?"

"Spooks, you know."

"No, spooks?"

"Yeah, spooks! Whooooaaahhhhh ... spooks ... ghosts ... Whooooahhhhh!"

"Ah, ghosts are spooks. I see! So a spook house is a ghost house, yes?"

"Right."

"And where is this spook house?"

David knew where to find Eric.

-- --

Eric Kruger came back to his senses. The pain in his chest was almost beyond bearing. A well of fresh blood oozed in the centre of his chest and spread on the thickening mat. He remembered the weapons. He removed Bishop's revolver from his left pocket and placed it on the floor beside him. He reached for the rifle at his side, dragging the weapon up so that it rested on his extended right leg. He gripped it between his knees and pulled back the bolt with a scrape and a sharp click of steel on steel. He loaded a shell from the magazine into the breech and lifted the rifle back onto his thigh. He curled a finger around the trigger and aimed the muzzle at the door. He lay back and closed his eyes.

-- --

David sucked in his breath as he saw the still-wet patch of blood on the Spook House door. *Knew it!* He reached out to pull the two loose boards open and stopped. His heart jumped at the sound of a motor vehicle coming to a stop, and a door banging and voices coming from the far side of the house.

He recognized Steve Roper's voice. "Go in slowly and cover a corner of the place each. If he got this far, he could easily have holed up. And keep an eye out for the kid."

David pulled the boards apart, flinching as they creaked. He slipped between them and stopped in the dark. His heart pounded wildly.

Maybe Eric wasn't really in here. Maybe he had just rested against the door and kept going.

He stretched out a hand in the blackness and gasped and jumped back as something touched his hand and moved away. He nearly screamed as the thing swung back at him, and he shot his hand up in defense. His fingers brushed a dangling, skimpy piece of string. *Too thin to hold a body!*

He heard boots crunching across the open space between the woods and the building, and heard Steve Roper cautioning, "Remember, he's hurt, but he's got weapons."

And Bishop's voice! "Don't give him any chance."

From somewhere overhead, David heard the click of metal against metal.

"Eric?" he called out in a loud whisper, and tried to stop the sound of the blood pumping in his ears. He groped in the dark, feeling with his feet as he shuffled further into the room. He made out the shape of the flight of stairs just as he made thudding contact with the bottom step.

He heard Roper from outside: "There! What was that? He's in there!"

And Bishop replying, "Well, go and get him out."

- -

The pain had almost gone. Kruger stared at the two people standing in a soft glow at the far doorway of a vast room, across which he seemed to have been walking for a long time. The taller one he realized was Michelle, in a halo of light. She smiled and reached out to him with open arms. Hans was at her side, laughing and beckoning to him. He felt as if he were growing lighter every second, as if at any moment he would be weightless.

There had been the occasional stop in the journey across the room. He had heard voices he knew, calling out names. He had heard David's voice. What a fine boy. Now there was another stop, and he did not care for this. He was going back. The light was receding. He could barely see Michelle and Hans. Please, God. He did not want this. But he was going back, and the pain had returned.

He was hunched in the dark corner, with the voices swimming in his head. One of them penetrated his reeling thoughts. Bishop! Bishop was out there, coming for him. He tightened his grip on the rifle, and with an effort he braced himself against the wall.

- -

At the foot of the stairs, David heard the movement in the room, above his head.

"Eric?" he whispered loudly. He climbed two of the steps, and called again. "Eric?"

Behind him, at the end of the building, the old plank door suddenly creaked and then snapped off its rusted hinges. A figure carrying a rifle ducked into the room and hugged the side wall.

"Eric!" David shouted, and he flew up the stairs, stumbling and falling flat as he hit the top landing.

Roper had seen David's slight figure moving in the sudden shaft of light as he entered the old house.

He yelled, "No! David! Stop! David!"

From outside, Bishop called, "Roper! What the hell is going on?"

\- -

Kruger heard the voices. They echoed and clattered around in his mind, with the last one repeating, "Roper!" It was Bishop's voice and Bishop was coming to get him, to punish him and torture him. He lifted the rifle, fighting off a massive wave of pain and nausea as blood seeped out of the wound and trickled down his chest. The voices raged in his fevered head and he aimed at the door.

\- -

At Roper's shout, David jumped to his feet on the landing. He threw himself at the closed door, smashing it open. He saw a dim figure propped against the wall in the far corner.

"Eric!" His triumphant shout echoed through the old building.

Roper had one foot on the bottom step when the rifle shot crashed out in the room above. He froze on the stairs. "Oh, Christ. Oh, my sweet Jesus Christ."

He started up the stairs, and was stopped by a cry from the room above, a tearing, animal sound of grief: "David! Daaaaaviiiid!"

Roper was almost at the top of the stairs when a second shot, from a lighter weapon, cracked the air.

\- -

Bishop glowered from his uninjured eye as Roper stepped through the damaged door and back into the sunlight.

"What's happened?"

Roper stared at him. "They're dead," he said. "Kruger's dead, and David Evans is dead. Kruger killed him. He can't have known."

Bishop's face went slack and his jowls quivered. "I ..."

"He must have thought it was you."

"What?"

"This time you went too far."

"Hey!" Bishop's eyes were swirling pools of fear. "Hey!"

chapter twenty-seven

Liz Thomas sat as if carved from stone while the room and its furnishing seemed to spin around her. She gripped the arm of the sofa and closed her eyes. The names ... *David Evans* ... *Ian Mackenzie* ... the ages ... the parents' names ... *beloved son of* ...

The only sound in the room was that of her own heartbeat. She exhaled slowly and opened her eyes., forcing her whirling thoughts to be still. She stared at the papers surrounding her on the sofa. Something ... yes, that one. She picked up the December 10, 1944 newspaper clipping with the story of the repatriations. Her brow creased. She went back into the batch of papers and thumbed through them until she found the creased form she had earlier put aside. It was a copy of a birth certificate, an official form of the Province of British Columbia in the name of Elizabeth Evans, female, born April 26, 1945, in Prince Rupert. She had known the name of her birthplace, a town on British Columbia's northwest coast, from asking her mother. She had no idea what her parents might have been doing there when she was born. When she'd asked, her mother just said, "We hadn't decided at that point where we were going to live. People moved around a lot after the war. Things were very unsettled." Liz stared at the document, puzzling, for some seconds. This was her birth certificate. But it was wrong. Her birthday was November 14. She opened a small envelope and took out a letter dated December 3, 1944. It was from the Department of National Defence in Ottawa, addressed to Kristin Evans at 42 Queen Street, Willow Creek, Alberta.

> Dear Mrs. Evans:
> We are pleased to forward advice from the
> International Red Cross that your husband,
> Lt. Gareth Evans of the King's Own Calgary
> Rifles, currently a prisoner of war in Bavaria,
> has been selected for repatriation. The decision
> has been made on medical grounds.

Lt. Evans is expected to leave from Marseille
in late December for New York from where he
will be escorted home.

The letter congratulated Mrs. Evans and offered good wishes for
the future for her and her returning husband, who had served his
country with honour.

It added that Lt. Evans would require an extended period of close
nursing care to assist in his convalescence once he was home.

chapter twenty-eight

Kristin had visited the cemetery every day since David and Ian were buried. Their graves were side by side with identical, slim granite markers. Flowers, both cultivated and wild, lay in neat bunches on both graves.

She touched David's headstone. A tear slipped from her cheek onto the grass, which was still crisp from the night's heavy frost. Any day now the graves would be hidden under a covering of snow.

She felt the letter in her pocket and shuddered.

The letter had arrived the day after the shootings. Kristin had wrestled with whether she would try to have Gareth informed of the loss of his son. She had decided against it and had asked the commanding officer of Military District 13 to honour her decision. She said she had no idea how seriously ill her husband was, nor what the shock of such news might do to his health.

"I'll deal with it when I have to," she said. That and the rest.

Oh, Christ, Gareth!

She flashed back to her conversation with Moira, when she had turned down her offer of a cigarette.

"What, you quit ...? Only time that happened with me was when I got pregnant. Soon as I caught, I couldn't stand the thought of a cigarette."

And to another conversation, with Steve Roper.

"I do not kiss and tell. Okay? Our secret."

Not for much longer. She was certain of the new life she was carrying. Roper hadn't used a contraceptive the second time they'd made love that day.

She knew there were places she could go, women who would "do something about it." She had thought about it. But there had been enough death. She was not going to cause another.

chapter twenty-nine

"You all right, love?"

She had not been aware that her husband Michael had entered the room.

"Liz?"

"Sorry," she said. "I was lost in this lot. I ..." She gestured to the papers and photographs.

Her father hadn't got back home until early 1945 and then he had needed an extended period of nursing care "to assist with his convalescence," so it likely would have been some time before her parents could have ...

Something wriggled at the back of her mind. She scuffled among the papers and picked up the letter from Moira.

> A few weeks before he died, he said he had
> something to tell me. I wish I had known
> at the time, Kristin! I wish you had told me
> so that I could have been some kind of help
> to you, if only as a friend to talk to. Which I
> always will be, a friend. You know it wouldn't
> have made any difference to me. When you
> went back east you said you needed to be
> there when Gareth landed, and I was look-
> ing forward to you both coming home. Then
> when the next letter came from Prince Rupert
> and you asked me if I wanted to buy the shop,
> I didn't know what to think. (Good job Steve
> was able to lend me the money—of course that
> loan became permanent!) It was after that that
> Morgan Evans showed up, saying the shop
> belonged to him. I showed him the letter, and
> the one where you confirmed receipt of the
> money and gave me the ownership. He said
> some terrible things, which I didn't under-
> stand then, but I'm glad to say I never saw
> him again.

> I guess I'm not surprised that Gareth
> decided he didn't want to see his family
> once you and he decided what to do. His life
> wouldn't have been worth living near that old
> b—. So you see, now I understand why you and
> Gareth moved away. I always thought it was
> just because of David.

Now she understood those looks of her father's. She remembered the times she had found Gareth looking at her with what seemed to be disappointment. She had mentioned it to her mother, wondering if maybe her father would have preferred to have had a son, and her mother had said, "No, it's just the way he is. His mind is often somewhere else. You have to remember that the war did strange things to people." She remembered her father telling her husband Michael in that strange tone, "I'll keep an eye on her." She shuddered at the thought of the darkness that must have festered in her father's soul for all those years.

There *had* been a son. Liz had a brother who had died. She picked up the wedding photo of Moira and Steve Roper. She stared at Roper's face. The green eyes, beneath blonde hair. A face she had seen many times before. In her mirror. Her father's face. She'd had a *half*-brother who had died.

Her mother and Steve Roper.

She picked up the small black-and-white group photo. David. Now the resemblance was unmistakable. She wondered how it must have been for her mother. Panic at first, probably, then fear, then resolution. Facing Gareth, and telling him first about David, and then about ... her.

She picked up the report and read the final paragraph.

Incident at Willow Creek:

Sgt. Major Bishop's condition has made it impossible for him to provide any further information concerning either the incident or his allegations against Cpl. Roper concerning Roper's "dealings" with the civilian population. (There is reason to believe, though no hard evidence to substantiate, that those allegations had substance to them.) The stroke that Bishop suffered when Roper's rifle discharged, wounding Bishop in the foot, has left him blind and incapable of communicating in any fashion.

Roper, as you are aware, claims the discharge was accidental and that
he was in shock after having witnessed the bodies of the boy and the
German. It would seem -- and I would recommend -- that the only charge
for which there is solid evidence against Roper is that of careless use of
a weapon.

Liz picked up Moira's last letter to Kristin and re-read a sentence
she had only skimmed earlier: "Steve got six months' detention
and was discharged. They should have given him a medal."

‐ ‐

Michael Thomas wore a patient smile as he watched his wife col-
lect the papers and photographs and place them in a neat pile.

When she had finished, he said, "So?"

"What?"

"I don't know. It's just that you've been so wrapped up in all
that." He gestured to the papers. "Like you've been in another
world. What's it all about?"

She looked across the room at her mother's photo on the sideboard. It seemed that the lines on Kristin Evans' face, deeper in her
later years, had been somehow smoothed away. The dark eyes held
a smile that Liz could not recall being there before. Liz shook her
head. No doubt it was just a trick of light in the late afternoon.

She turned to her husband.

"Pour us both a drink, then come and sit down."

acknowledgements

I am grateful to Mrs. Pat Powers, formerly of the Lethbridge Public Library, who patiently guided me through descriptions of life in small-town Alberta at the time in which this novel is set, and through the archived files of the *Lethbridge Herald* and other Alberta newspapers. Thanks also to my editor, Lynne Van Luven, for her incisive observations and welcome suggestions, and to NeWest Marketing and Production Coordinator Tiffany Regaudie for her relentless energy in keeping this book on track and on time.

I would also like to thank Canadian author John Melady, whose book *Escape from Canada!* provided me with information about the day-to-day operations of Canada's (German) POW camps: Who could have known that at least one set of talented German POWs in Alberta formed their own symphony orchestra—with instruments bought through the Eaton's catalogue?

Don Hunter emigrated from the UK to Canada in 1961, where he earned a B.Ed from the University of British Columbia. In 1969 he joined *The Province*, a daily newspaper in Vancouver, as a theatre critic, reporter, editor, and eventually as a writer for the upfront opinion column "Out and About." A personal memoir of his teaching experiences in northern BC led to a CBC television movie and a subsequent mini-series drama in 1989. That same year, his collection of short stories, *Spinner's Inlet*, was shortlisted for the Stephen Leacock Prize.

Hunter currently lives in Fort Langley, BC, with his wife, June. They are the parents of two daughters, Susan and Taryn.

The production of the title *Incident at Willow Creek* on Rolland Enviro 100 Print paper instead of virgin fibres paper reduces your ecological footprint by :

Tree(s) : 6
Solid waste : 359 lb
Water : 3,390 gal
Suspended particles in the water : 2,3 lb
Air emissions : 789 lb
Natural gas : 822 ft^3

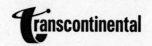

   100%   PERMANENT

Printed on Rolland Enviro 100, containing 100% post-consumer recycled fibers, Eco-Logo certified, Processed without chlorinate, FSC Recycled and manufactured using biogas energy.